Viktoria wasn't sure who she had been expecting, but she had never imagined this.

His handshake was firm. His skin was cool, but she wasn't ... heat that spread from his finger... ...rm. She managed ... while her skin ... ...ch.

She waited for hi... ...meet her, but he didn't. Was that so... ...e only said to be polite?

"I understand you wanted to see the games facilities," he said as he released her hand.

She nodded. The power of speech had deserted her momentarily. Dr. Campbell Hamilton was tall, dark and handsome and made her feel strangely nervous.

She had an odd sensation that this man was the reason she was here. That he was what she'd come for. She had an overpowering sense that he was going to play an important role in her days here. Or was she just getting caught up in the excitement of the day ahead?

Dear Reader,

I am so excited to share Viktoria and Cam's story with you. This is the first time I've written a romance featuring a princess and I can see why they are so popular—bringing Viktoria to life was a lot of fun.

When Princess Viktoria needed to escape her life of royal duty, expectation and close scrutiny, Sydney seemed like the perfect place to send her. As a rule, Australians are not really that fussed about royalty, so sending the princess down under gave her a chance to experience a normal life for a while. But she hadn't counted on meeting Dr. Campbell Hamilton, an army medic who is battling his own demons.

The idea for this story has been with me for a while, but I needed time to get my characters right and work out how to bring a damaged Australian army vet who is committed to his job and a European princess together. I hope I have done them justice.

I'd love to hear from you if you enjoyed this story or any of my others. You can visit my website at emily-forbesauthor.com or drop me a line at emilyforbes@internode.on.net.

Emily

THE ARMY DOC'S
SECRET PRINCESS

——

EMILY FORBES

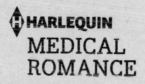

HARLEQUIN®
MEDICAL ROMANCE™

Recycling programs for this product may not exist in your area.

ISBN-13: 978-1-335-14957-2

The Army Doc's Secret Princess

Copyright © 2020 by Emily Forbes

This edition published by arrangement with Harlequin Books S.A.

For questions and comments about the quality of this book, please contact us at CustomerService@Harlequin.com.

Harlequin Enterprises ULC
22 Adelaide St. West, 40th Floor
Toronto, Ontario M5H 4E3, Canada
www.Harlequin.com

Printed in U.S.A.

Emily Forbes is an award-winning author of Harlequin Medical Romance novels. She has written over twenty-five books and has twice been a finalist in the Australian Romantic Book of the Year Award, which she won in 2013 for her novel *Sydney Harbor Hospital: Bella's Wishlist*. You can get in touch with Emily at emilyforbes@internode.on.net or visit her website at emily-forbesauthor.com.

Books by Emily Forbes

Harlequin Medical Romance

London Hospital Midwives
Reunited by Their Secret Daughter

Nurses in the City
Reunited with Her Brooding Surgeon

The Christmas Swap
Waking Up to Dr. Gorgeous

Tempted & Tamed
A Doctor by Day…
Tamed by the Renegade
A Mother to Make a Family

One Night That Changed Her Life
Falling for His Best Friend
Rescued by the Single Dad
Taming Her Hollywood Playboy

Visit the Author Profile page
at Harlequin.com for more titles.

For dearest Xander and Mel,
congratulations to you as you celebrate
your wedding day
and your commitment to each other.

Xander, make sure you treat Mel like a princess!

Mel, please take care of my nephew.

Wishing you both a lifetime of happily-ever-afters.

With all my love,
Auntie Emily

**Praise for
Emily Forbes**

"Ms. Forbes has delivered a delightful read in
this book where emotions run high because of
everything this couple go through on their journey
to happy ever after…and where the chemistry
between this couple was strong; the romance
was delightful and had me loving these two
together…."

—*Harlequin Junkie* on
Rescued by the Single Dad

PROLOGUE

Two years ago

CAMPBELL'S HEADPHONES BLOCKED out most of the engine noise, but he could still hear a faint rhythmic thump-thump as the chopper blades beat the air and he could feel the vibrations as they shuddered through his body. After almost six months he thought he'd be used to the overwhelming assault on his senses—the smell of fumes and dust, the incessant noise, the constant jarring and jolting—but he had yet to get used to the tension. He was always on edge when he was in flight, despite knowing that one of the Australian Army's best pilots was in control of the aircraft, and he was looking forward to getting back on the ground.

Cam kept his eyes cast down, focusing on his patient. He kept up a one-sided conversation despite the fact that his patient was heavily sedated, and the engine noise would make conversation almost impossible even if he were conscious. He gave him a rundown of his situation—only the positives though. His IV line was running smoothly and his vital signs had stabilised, he told him. He avoided the specifics of his injuries. The soldier was badly wounded, but he didn't need to be reminded of that. He'd live, at this stage that was the important information, but he'd be getting sent home for a while. Home to Australia. Where he'd have a chance to recover physically, if not mentally.

Cam knew the soldiers would always be haunted by their experiences fighting a war on the other side of the world. Some would cope better than others. He knew he'd have scars too. Mental, not physical. This war wasn't what he'd anticipated or expected.

Gemma had warned him, but how did you warn someone who had grown up in rural Australia? A land of dust and dirt but safe enough. Hot, and at times desolate, but it had been a different sort of barren. A different sort of danger.

Apart from the snakes and some angry rams or falling off a motorbike or a horse, Cam hadn't really had anything to worry about. Now, every day was a battle. Here, there was always a chance of getting hit by a bullet, being on the wrong side of an IED, being wounded or killed by enemy fire or even by a civilian on a suicide mission. Life here was stressful.

His job as a medical specialist with the Australian Army meant he was responsible for lives in a country where lives were not highly regarded. Lives here were seen as disposable, which went against everything he believed in and made his job difficult and, at times, impossible. He still had access to First World medical facilities but, more often than not, he was trying to save lives in the middle of a dust bowl, trying to do his best while war raged around him. Gemma had tried to explain it to him but, until he'd seen it with his own eyes, until he'd lived through the experiences she had told him about, he knew he hadn't understood.

He glanced towards the cockpit to where Gemma sat in the pilot's seat. As if she had felt his gaze, his fiancée turned and looked back at him and smiled.

Cam was looking forward to getting back to base. He was looking forward to dinner with Gemma, even if it was just in the mess tent. He could pretend for a moment that they were a normal couple, looking forward to making a life together, planning a family. He needed that idea of his future—it was what kept him going on tough days. Gemma was the bright spot in his world. He loved his job but, if he was asked, he'd have to admit he preferred to do his job in the sterile environment of an Australian medical facility. He didn't mind dust and dirt, he was country born and bred after all, but practising medicine in these conditions was challenging, often unpleasant and definitely not fun.

But no one was interested in his opinion and if he wanted to be with Gemma, this was where she was.

He wondered if he had any chance of convincing her to quit the army and return to Australia. She loved flying but it would be years before she would achieve flight instructor status with the army. Years before she wouldn't have to fly combat missions. Perhaps she could work privately instead.

He wondered when it would be safe to have that discussion. Would it ever? Could he ask her to give up something she loved? How would he feel if she started to tell him how to live his life or run his career?

He knew he wouldn't be happy.

He blew her a kiss just as a bright light burst in his peripheral vision.

The chopper lurched as Gemma's head whipped around and even through the headphones Cam could hear the sound of tearing metal.

The chopper shuddered and he could see Gemma and her co-pilot fighting to keep control as the bird started to spin.

It took him a few seconds to work out what had happened. It felt like an eternity.

They'd been hit.

There was a second explosion, the burst of light so intense that Cam closed his eyes against the glare.

He could feel the chopper spinning wildly. He opened his eyes and saw the ground rushing towards them as the machine fell from the sky.

Black smoke filled the cabin, making Cam's eyes water. He couldn't see Gemma. He couldn't see anything. He lost all sense of space and time.

He threw himself over his patient as the helicopter plummeted. He knew it was a ridiculous gesture. He wasn't going to be able to protect him. He wasn't going to be able to save him. The situation was completely out of his control.

There was nothing he could do.

* * *

Cam's eyes flickered open.

His head was pounding and he closed his eyes again as he fought back a wave of nausea. His ears were ringing and there was a metallic taste in his mouth. Blood.

He licked his lip. It was split and swollen but the blood was still wet. He was dazed, disoriented but he knew then that he hadn't been knocked out for long.

He opened his eyes and looked around the cabin. Acrid smoke still billowed in the air, making his eyes water and obscuring his vision.

He breathed in through his nose, trying to avoid getting a mouthful of smoke. A sharp pain speared through the left side of his chest, making him gasp with pain. His breathing was shallow, restricted.

He lifted one hand to his chest and pressed gently under his armpit. His ribs screamed in protest even as he subconsciously registered that his left arm still functioned. That was good. He had obviously fractured some ribs, but it appeared that he hadn't sustained major damage to his upper spine at least.

He could feel pain in his right hip as well as his ribs, but he knew that sometimes pain was a good thing; it meant his nerve endings were intact. Sometimes even a painful sensation was better than no sensation.

The smoke was acrid but, underlying the smoke, Cam could smell fumes. That focused his attention.

They needed to get out of the chopper.

Would it explode? How long did they have?

Who had fired the missile at them? And where were they? Were they close? Or perhaps far enough away that they hadn't seen the distinctive red cross marking the bird as a medical transport? Or perhaps they didn't care?

The inside of the chopper was dark. The faint glow of green emergency lights gave an eerie aspect, failing to pierce the smoky interior. Visibility was poor but the cabin was also quiet. He couldn't hear a sound. Was everyone else still unconscious? Or worse?

The smoke began to clear, and Cam peered around the cabin. The stretcher that had held his patient was on its side. Crumpled. He was sure he'd thrown himself over his patient, but the force of the impact had thrown him against the opposite wall of the chopper.

He looked to the front of the chopper.

There was a gaping hole where Gemma's seat should be.

'Gemma!'

Pain shot through his chest again. He was out of breath and his voice was raspy. Hoarse. His tongue felt thick and his swollen lip deformed his words.

'Gemma!'

He had to move but he knew it was going to hurt. He pressed his right hand against his ribs, trying to hold them together as he grabbed the side of the chopper with his left hand. He tried to keep his left elbow pressed against his side, pressing against his right hand, but still his ribs protested and his vision blurred with pain. Little black dots danced in front of his eyes and he blinked, trying to clear them away as he pulled himself to his feet. He made it into a semi-upright position, leaning through his right side, but the moment he put his weight onto his right foot an intense pain shot through his pelvis.

His right leg refused to take his weight. It wouldn't hold.

It gave way beneath him as searing pain tore through him.

He collapsed, Gemma's name still on his lips, as everything went black.

CHAPTER ONE

Present day

CAMPBELL'S LEG ACHED and he fought hard against the urge to stand up. The meeting had been long and he was beginning to get restless. He'd never been good at sitting still and these days it was almost impossible. He needed to stand and stretch; prolonged periods of sitting disagreed with him. Irritated his mind and his body. If he sat still his leg complained and his mind wandered. He needed to be moving, he needed to be busy. He wanted to keep his mind occupied. He didn't want time to dwell. Too much time to think had proven to be difficult.

He stretched his right leg out under the boardroom table as he tried to ease the cramp in his hip. He needed to get in the pool. Swim a few laps. He would prefer to swim a few laps in the ocean, but he knew from experience that he'd fare better in a warm pool. The heated water would ease his aching muscles. It had been two years since the chopper crash and he didn't need ice baths any more.

It had been twenty-four months since the incident, but he was still adjusting to his new life.

A life as a solitary man.

'Any other problems?'

He brought his attention back to the meeting as Douglas began to wrap it up.

Thank goodness it was almost over. Cam hoped no one had any additional items for discussion. He looked around the table at the ten other men and women, trying to gauge if any of them looked like they had something on their mind. He'd had enough experience with meetings, ward rounds as well as military discussion groups, to know that there was always one person who seemed to delight in dragging meetings on for far too long but today, for once, it appeared as though everyone was just as eager to escape as he was.

He stood up the minute Douglas officially closed the meeting. He stretched, knowing that if he didn't take a moment to ease the stiffness in his back and leg his limp would be far more pronounced, and he preferred not to draw attention to himself.

He was used to being noticed but he didn't want to be noticed for the wrong reasons. He knew that was ironic and he'd never say it out loud, not when he was surrounded by so many others with far more severe disabilities and injuries than he had, but he knew that perception was a very personal thing.

'You okay?' Doug was beside him.

Cam knew Doug would have noticed his attempt at surreptitious stretching. Doug was one of his closest friends in the service and had been a good support to him during his rehabilitation and recovery phase. His family and friends had helped get him through the past year. He felt he owed it to them to pull through, although there had been times when it had seemed like too much effort, but he was having better days now.

He knew he'd been difficult. He'd been the sole survivor of the incident that had claimed the lives of five others, including his fiancée. He'd been angry but he'd eventually managed to let go of that anger; however, guilt had continued to eat away at him. It still did. He knew the incident hadn't been his fault but the fact he hadn't been able to save anyone, especially Gemma, was hard to live with and it remained an effort to get through his days with a smile.

Work had been his saviour. Initially he hadn't wanted to listen to other people's problems but gradually he'd found that if he focused on their issues it gave him less time to think about his own. Keeping busy had been the key and now he threw himself into whatever came his way and he had taken on all manner of tasks in the past twelve months since returning to his post as an army medic.

'Yes,' he replied, 'just too many meetings.' His need to keep busy was what had landed him in this situation in the first place. 'When I agreed to be the medical liaison officer on the committee, I didn't expect to spend so much time in discussions. I expected my role to be in an advisory capacity.'

His pain made him grumpy. He knew it. He should take some painkillers, but he needed the strong ones and he needed to keep a clear head. He needed his wits about him; he didn't want to get roped into any more committees or be given any more tasks to do. He had enough on his plate.

'It is.'

'Well, then, I didn't think it was possible to have this many meetings.' Cam had made no secret of the fact that he liked to be busy and when he'd agreed to be on this committee he'd imagined that he'd be doing something practical like overseeing the medical facilities and programme for the games, not sitting around in meetings.

'We're almost done,' Doug said, making an effort to appease him. He knew full well Cam's opinion about meetings. 'The Games start next week.'

The countdown was on until the Legion's Games began, when hundreds of injured veterans from twenty countries around the world would descend on Sydney to compete in a dozen different events across ten days. The Games were the brainchild of Prince Alfred, an army captain himself, and the Games Committee was responsible for the event but, as the host nation, the Australian defence force was heavily involved. It was a massive exercise and the logistics of the Games fell to the Australians, which was how Cam found himself involved.

'Not much longer and your suffering will all be over,' Doug added with a smile.

Cam doubted that. Sure, he'd have fewer meetings to attend but his current life was still so far removed from what he'd thought it was going to be; he wasn't sure that his suffering was ever going to be over.

He'd hoped the Games would be a good distraction, a way to mark the passing of time. He'd expected to be consulted over the details of the medical facilities, but somehow, he'd found himself dragged along to every damn meeting in existence. He tried to be positive. He'd put his hand up for this project after all, but he'd put his hand up for any work that had been offered to him over the past year. Exhaustion was the only way he could get even a half-decent night's sleep. A few hours when he could shut out the horrors of everything he'd experienced during his tour of duty in the Middle East.

'What are your plans for tonight?' Doug asked as they left the boardroom together, Cam's muscles finally relaxing enough to enable him to walk without a limp. Well, without much of a limp.

'I'm going to head to the pool.'

'You're not seeing that girl from the other night? What was her name?'

'Caroline,' Cam said, before adding, 'no.'

He'd been on a few dates recently, if you could call them that. Dates that had been set up through his friends in the armed forces. Dates with girls who were happy to have a night out. But not one of them had progressed further than a single night. Not one had ended in anything more than a kiss. Cam was scarred, physically and emotionally, and he wasn't ready to expose himself to anyone new. He wasn't ready for those conversations. He wasn't interested in having a relationship.

He wasn't short of female attention; he knew women considered him good-looking, and while the copper crash had shattered his femur and fractured his pelvis his face had remained relatively unscathed. He had a small scar running through his bottom lip but otherwise his facial features were unmarked.

He wasn't lacking female attention, but his heart remained hardened. He wasn't interested in getting to know any of them in detail and he definitely did not want them getting to know him. He didn't want to answer questions about himself. He didn't want to open up, to share his thoughts and feelings. He wanted to lock the pain away.

He disagreed with the psychologists. Talking about what had happened only made the pain worse. It only kept the memory alive. Made it stronger. No one, least of all Cam, needed to be reminded of what had happened.

'Well, before you go, can I have a word with you about tomorrow's schedule?' Doug asked.

'Don't tell me there are more meetings—I'm consulting tomorrow and I know my list is pretty full.'

'I know you're out at the rehab centre tomorrow; that's why I need to speak to you. I have a favour to ask. The Prince's social media manager has arrived in Sydney ahead of the Prince and has asked for a tour of the facilities.'

'Which facilities?'

'All of them. But I thought we could start with the old barracks first.'

One of the old inner-city army bases had been repurposed as a rehabilitation facility when the site had needed updating. The active units had been reassigned to a new purpose-built base in the outer suburbs of Sydney and the old base had been upgraded and was now home to the medical facilities, including doctors, physiotherapists, psychologists, exercise physiologists, a purpose-built gym and pool for the injured and returned soldiers, along with outdoor sporting facilities. The repurposed base was going to serve as the venue for the majority of the events in the Legion's Games.

'You're out there tomorrow,' Doug continued. 'Can they go out there with you?'

'You want me to babysit the Prince's— what did you call them—social media manager?'

Doug nodded and sweetened the deal. 'If you can do me this small favour, I promise I won't drag you into any meetings for the rest of the week.'

Cam sighed and ran his hand through his thick, dark hair. A day out of the boardroom was preferable to another day of meetings. Even playing tour guide to a stranger would have to be better than that. 'All right,' he agreed.

'Okay, I'll send you the details,' Doug said as he took out his phone and tapped away. 'Can you collect her from her hotel at o-nine hundred hours?'

'Her?' he asked as his phone pinged with the incoming email. Prince Alfred had a military background and Cam had, incorrectly it seemed, assumed his social media manager would be a man.

Cam had met the Prince once while he'd been deployed in the Middle East. Once, in the days before the incident. In the days before his life went down the toilet.

'Yes—' Doug grinned '—see if you can dredge up some of your old charm. Be nice.'

Cam looked at the email on his screen and noted her name, along with the hotel address, with a raised eyebrow. Apparently, Viktoria von Grasburg was staying in one of Sydney's five-star hotels on the Harbour. He wondered who was paying for that.

'Sure,' he said as he sighed and stuck his phone back in his pocket, before massaging his hip subconsciously.

Viktoria woke up well before sunrise as her body clock still hadn't adjusted to the Australian time zone. She rolled over and picked up her phone, knowing she wouldn't get back to sleep. She had plenty of time to kill so she opened her emails and was relieved to find nothing important. Out of habit, she googled her name and then wished she hadn't.

Another name popped up in the feed. Luca Romano. The successful, handsome captain of Italy's national polo team and her ex-fiancé. She knew his name would always be linked to hers—as a princess, she was a popular topic for the European media and her tumultuous love life was considered headline news. And nothing was more interesting in the world of 'entertainment' news than a royal scandal.

She'd thought Luca was her perfect man—strong and handsome with enough confidence to cope with the expectations of the public and the palace. But he'd turned out to be just another person who was more interested in fame and fortune—his fame and her fortune—than in settling down into a monogamous relationship. And loyalty and trust were two things Viktoria was not prepared to compromise on.

Luca had cheated on her and made sure she found out. As a defence he said he'd wanted to save her the embarrassment of being dumped by making it impossible for her to forgive him. He'd *wanted* her to break off their engagement but even though she had been able to end their relationship it had still hurt her. More than she would ever let on. She'd been taught to hold her head high in public but that hadn't lessened the pain she'd felt in private.

Three months later Luca was free now to do as he pleased and, by the look of the woman on his arm, he was enjoying his freedom. She knew she was better off without him in her life; she just wished she had the same freedom. She wished she could do as she pleased.

She closed the browser and put her phone down, sighing as she swung her legs out of bed. In a way Luca was responsible for her ending up here, in Sydney.

She was in Australia to have a break from her royal duties, a break from the tabloids constantly following her disastrous love life, and she was determined to enjoy her anonymity and associated freedom.

Her freedom would end soon enough, once she returned to Berggrun. She accepted that; it was the promise she had made to her parents. Berggrun princes and princesses were expected to marry by the age of thirty—to marry and start producing heirs to the throne. It was a tradition and the only way of ensuring the tiny principality didn't disappear. The timeline had been pushed out by her father but, even so, the deadline was looming for Viktoria. She would turn thirty next year and, while she might not be married, she would be expected to be engaged. She hadn't managed to hold on to her fiancé and she knew her parents had a shortlist of eligible potential husbands. By the time she returned home she expected her fate would have been decided. The next two weeks were her last chance of freedom.

She pressed the button on the remote to open the curtains. She stood up and gazed out of the window, refusing to let her future issues ruin what looked to be another glorious day. The sun had risen in the east and the endless sky was duck-egg-blue, broken only by a few wisps of white cloud. The water of Sydney Harbour sparkled in the early morning light and the Harbour Bridge looked almost close enough to touch, looming large outside the floor-to-ceiling windows of her penthouse suite.

Well, she reminded herself as she watched the boats scurrying across the water, today was the first day of the rest of her life. For the next couple of weeks, she was free from the constraints of being a royal and she was going to make the most of it. She was in Australia to do something worthwhile, something meaningful, and she was damn certain she would give it her best shot. She didn't have time to dwell on ex-fiancés, future husbands or even her life as a royal from the House of von Grasburg. This was her opportunity to be something other than a princess.

She headed for the shower as she thought about the conversation she'd had eight weeks ago with her cousin Freddie, when she'd flown to London to join in his thirtieth birthday celebrations. The two of them, and their siblings, had a close relationship but at that moment in time Viktoria had felt the gap between their lives very strongly. She'd been very aware of the immense divide between their lives and their futures. Freddie and his siblings had grown up in England—his mother was her father's sister—and Viktoria had always envied their more relaxed royal protocols. While they were expected to fill their days with meaningful pursuits—Freddie had served in the British army and had founded a charity he was passionate about—they weren't governed by the same strict traditions. Unlike her, Freddie was not expected to marry by the age of thirty.

'So,' he had said to her two months ago, 'my parents were telling me that yours are busy narrowing down the list of potential husbands for you.'

'Do not remind me,' Viktoria had groaned. 'I cannot believe it has come down to this. I cannot believe I thought Luca and I were going to live happily ever after. I cannot believe I am in this situation.'

'Do you have any idea who the options are?'

'I know my parents have mentioned a count from eastern Europe and also Tomas, the Duke of San Fernando.'

'Do you have a preference?'

'Tomas, I guess. At least I know him.' Part of her still imagined she'd find her true love before she ran out of time, but she knew she wasn't being realistic.

'Let's hope, for your sake, your parents make better decisions than you did. What *are* your plans for your last few months of freedom?'

'I wish I knew. I imagine it will be the usual list of functions. I don't mind the charity work but I am not looking forward to a life of service. I am tired of handing out awards and trophies and making small talk with a smile. All I seem to do is open museums and visit schools and hospitals. I want to feel like I am making a difference, not just decorating an event. I would like a break from being a royal for a while, but I cannot see that happening.'

That was the problem. She was jealous of other people, who could reinvent themselves or do as they pleased. People who could change their mind without having to ask for permission. She'd never been able to make independent decisions about anything ever. And after ten years as an adult that was beginning to get mighty frustrating.

'But, to be honest, I would really rather stay out of the spotlight. It would be nice to think I could experience life as an ordinary person before I am married off. You had your time in the army, when people treated you like a soldier, not a prince. You told me how much that meant to you. I want that. Maybe I should come to Sydney with you.'

Freddie, or Prince Alfred as he was known to most of the world, had been a captain in the armed forces and was the founder and patron of the Legion's Games, which was about to be staged for the third time in Sydney. The event was designed to inspire recovery and aid rehabilitation for service men and women in the armed forces through the healing power of sport. It was Freddie's brainchild and something he was passionate about. Viktoria envied him that passion and was in awe of the fact that he had been able to create something that would have a lasting legacy. She knew her work as a royal was important for the small principality of Berggrun, but she couldn't honestly say she was changing the world. She knew she was unlikely to ever make a significant difference but she'd like the opportunity to find out what she was capable of, rather than being instructed in how to live her life, how to behave, and directed to what tasks she could undertake, which duties were considered suitable for a princess.

She was passionate about horses but that was a personal passion and she had no idea how to make that something she could share with the world. She wasn't sure what she would do if she was given free rein, but she wished she'd have an opportunity to find out.

'Maybe you should,' he replied.

She had made an off-the-cuff comment but Freddie had taken her seriously.

'Really?'

'You could come to Australia as part of my team.'

'And do what?' she asked, tempted by the idea of travelling to Australia. Being on the other side of the planet sounded pretty good to her right now.

'I'm not sure exactly, but surely we could find something that could use that marketing and public relations degree you got at university. Maybe you could run the social media accounts for the Games and liaise with the press? Sort of like a marketing exercise. You could sell the Games to the general public. We could use this as an opportunity to promote the benefits that sport can make to physical and mental health. How does that sound?'

'I want to be anonymous for a while; I do not want to be part of the royal entourage.'

'You could simply be an employee. No one needs to know you're my cousin. Trust me, most Australians don't care about royalty. I swear most of them only make a fuss because they think it's expected. Don't forget I spent a year there at boarding school when I was fifteen. They only cared about my sporting skills, whether I was any good at cricket and rugby, not about whether I lived in a palace. They couldn't have cared less.'

'They know you.'

'That's because they're still part of the Commonwealth so they have a direct connection to me through the Crown, but I doubt many of them would have heard of the Principality of Berggrun. If they ever knew my mother was a Berggruner I'm sure they've forgotten that by now and I bet most Australians would never have heard of you.'

Viktoria laughed for the first time that day. 'You sure know how to make a girl feel special, Freddie.'

'You can't have it both ways, Viktoria,' her cousin teased her. 'You might want to be anonymous, but you know your parents have to give their approval if you want to run away. You need a valid reason to skip off to the other side of the world. This way, I can speak to Uncle Georg and make it sound official. Believe me, you won't regret it. Think about it and let me know. I guarantee you'll love it.'

Viktoria hadn't had to think about it for long. It wasn't as if she had anything better to do. Her parents and brothers could manage any royal engagements for two weeks. Handing out trophies was hardly challenging.

She was on the other side of the world and, she thought as she turned off the shower, she was about to start her first day 'on the job'. One that had nothing to do with her being a royal, a princess. Nothing to do with cutting ribbons, shaking hands or making speeches. She was working for her cousin, the Prince, but no one in Australia actually knew who she was. No one here knew she was a princess. As far as the organisers of the Legion's Games were concerned she was just running the Prince's social media campaign.

Freddie had told her no one would be bothered anyway but she hadn't believed him. She was about to find out.

She wrapped the soft white towelling robe around her and stepped out of the bathroom to find her assistant waiting for her. Viktoria's father had given permission for her to travel to Sydney with the proviso that she was escorted. Brigitta was on hand to attend to her schedule, wardrobe, hair and make-up. They had known each other since they were children—Brigitta's mother worked in the palace too—and Viktoria had to admit she was pleased to have some familiar company. As eager as she'd been to escape the palace, she wasn't accustomed to being alone.

'Can you run me through the plans for the day?' she asked as she noticed the outfit Brigitta had chosen and laid out on the bed for her.

She was confident she knew what was on the agenda, but she knew that plans could change at the last minute and she didn't want to be caught out. It was important to her to give a good first impression.

'One of the Games officials will meet you here at nine o'clock and escort you out to the facilities,' Brigitta told her. 'I gather most of the events will take place at one main venue and you'll tour that first.'

Viktoria planned to take some photographs throughout the day and start tweeting some inspirational messages to get the competitors psyched for the start of the Games and to catch the public's attention too. She looked at the outfit Brigitta had laid out for her again. A dress with a full skirt, wide straps and buttons running down the front was paired with wedge-heeled sandals. The irony that she'd wanted freedom to make her own decisions yet was still happy for Brigitta to select her clothes was not lost on her.

'Do you think I could wear something a little more casual?' she asked. 'It sounds like I could be doing a lot of walking. Flat shoes maybe?' She could tell by Brigitta's raised eyebrows that she had confounded her. Viktoria's mother, the Princess, *never* approved flat shoes but Viktoria wasn't going to let her mother's fashion sense dictate her wardrobe from the other side of the world. 'I imagine I'll be spending the day with a

lot of people in uniform,' she argued, before
Brigitta could protest, 'I do not want to look
overdressed.' Besides, she'd worn flat shoes
yesterday when she and Brigitta had played
tourists, but she knew that was different. She
wasn't pretending to work then.

'What did you have in mind?'

'I am not sure,' she said, realising that
she really had no idea but knowing that she
wanted the freedom to make the decision,
'but I am definitely thinking flat shoes.
What about those trainers I wore yesterday?'

They had spent yesterday morning wan-
dering around the historic Rocks area adjacent the hotel before heading down to the
wildlife park on Darling Harbour. They'd
been accompanied by Hendrik, a member
of her family's security team who doubled
as a driver and had also been sent to Australia by Viktoria's father. She wished she
and Brigitta had been permitted to venture
out alone, but she knew better than to sug-
gest it. Hendrik would never allow it. Instead
she'd tried to get Hendrik to blend in, to give
the impression that they were three friends
travelling together as opposed to a princess,
her security guard and her personal assistant. She wasn't sure how successful they'd
been, but no one had seemed to recognise

her so maybe Freddie was right. Maybe she would get some freedom here in Sydney.

Brigitta disappeared into the walk-in closet and emerged with a pair of Viktoria's white jeans, white leather sneakers, a navy blazer and a selection of lightweight camisoles. 'Something like this?'

'Perfect,' Viktoria said as she chose a patterned camisole and dressed quickly before sitting down to let Brigitta attend to her hair.

'What are you going to do today?' Viktoria asked as Brigitta brushed her thick, pale blonde hair before styling it in a loose plait that fell over one shoulder.

'I think I'll have to go shopping if you're going to insist on changing up your outfits. One pair of flat shoes is not going to see you through the next two weeks,' she said with a smile as she started applying Viktoria's make-up. She kept it simple, applying light foundation to Viktoria's creamy skin, highlighting her cheekbones with blush and using mascara and eyeliner to frame her blue eyes. As she finished coating Viktoria's lips with gloss the hotel telephone rang.

'There's a Dr Campbell Hamilton here to escort you,' Brigitta told Viktoria once she answered. 'I'll message Hendrik, tell him you're ready,' she said as she handed Viktoria a small bag. 'I've put your phone, a credit card, a make-up purse and your sunglasses in there. Your schedule is on your phone.'

Viktoria took a deep breath to calm her nerves, suddenly realising this was it. She was doing this. Going off to work like a regular person, out into the world.

She took the lift down to Reception. She stepped out, wondering how she would know who to look for, before realising the reception staff would advise her. She looked to the front desk and her attention was caught by a man in army uniform standing near the concierge.

'Miss von Grasburg?' he addressed her, and she was momentarily flummoxed. She wasn't used to being addressed so casually. There was no *Your Highness* or even *ma'am*.

No, this was what she wanted, she reminded herself. He knew all he needed to know. She smiled to herself and swallowed her surprise.

She was Miss von Grasburg.

CHAPTER TWO

'PLEASE, CALL ME VIKTORIA,' she said as she nodded and held out her hand to shake his.

'Campbell Hamilton.'

He was tall, over six feet, with thick dark hair which was a little longer than she thought would meet standard army regulations. He looked lean and muscular, fit without being too bulky. He had wide blue-grey eyes and a dimpled chin. He was clean-shaven with a full mouth and she could see a small scar running through his bottom lip. He was handsome. Very handsome.

She wasn't sure who she had been expecting but she had never imagined this.

His handshake was firm, his skin cool, but she wasn't prepared for the heat that spread from his fingertips into her hand and up her arm. She managed to maintain her composure even while her skin tingled and flared under his touch.

She waited for him to say it was a pleasure to meet her, but he didn't. Was that something people only said to be polite?

'I understand you want to see the Games facilities?' he said as he released her hand.

She nodded. The power of speech had deserted her momentarily. Dr Campbell Hamilton was tall, dark and handsome and made her feel strangely nervous.

She had an odd sensation that this man was the reason she was here. That he was what she'd come for. She had an overpowering sense that he was going to play an important role in her days here. Or was she just getting caught up in the excitement of the day ahead?

'My car is out the front,' he said as he turned and began walking towards the exit. He was quite abrupt, and Viktoria was a little thrown. While she had the sense that he was important, that there was some sort of connection between them, he didn't appear to share her thoughts. She got the impression she had annoyed him. He seemed to wish he was somewhere else. Doing something else. Her bubble of enthusiasm deflated slightly but, refusing to be completely crushed, she followed him outside.

He was standing beside a white SUV, holding the door open for her.

She hesitated.

'Is there a problem?' he asked when she made no move to climb in.

Viktoria looked down the driveway and saw Hendrik pulling to a stop in the driveway.

'I arranged for Hendrik to drive us,' she said.

'Who?'

She gestured towards the black luxury SUV that was now stationary behind Campbell's car. 'Hendrik. My driver.'

'You have a driver?'

'*Oui.*'

'No one said anything about a driver. This is my car. I will be driving.'

Viktoria made a split decision. She didn't want to irritate him further and she wanted to live like a normal person. She'd let him drive. That would be safe enough, surely? After all, he was a government employee. 'Do you have some identification?' she asked.

'Identification?' He was frowning.

'*Oui.* If you can show Hendrik some identification to verify yourself, I will give him the day off and let you drive me.' She knew

Hendrik wouldn't be happy, but she'd deal with him later.

'You'll *let* me drive you?'

His tone was frosty, but Viktoria nodded even as she wished they could begin this conversation again. They were not getting off to a great start.

Cam bit back a sigh and resisted the urge to run his hand through his hair in frustration. He should have taken the meetings. This was going to be a nightmare. They already seemed to be at cross purposes, working off different briefs. He couldn't care less if she came with him or not, but he had gone out of his way to collect her this morning and he didn't appreciate finding out that it hadn't been necessary. He could have easily met her at the barracks and sorted out her credentials and visitor's clearance then. But he knew he had to be polite. This woman worked for the Prince. It wouldn't do to get her offside. He suspected she was going to be demanding. She probably had every right to be, but he wished he wasn't going to be the one who had to meet her demands.

And then she smiled at him.

The photo provided for her clearance documents hadn't done her justice. It had been a

flattering photo—she'd looked attractive—
but he'd been mistaken. She wasn't just
pretty; she was absolutely stunning.

Her smile was like the sun coming out
and it burnt through the fog that had surrounded his psyche for the past two years.
As the fog lifted, he felt as if he could see
clearly for the first time in months...and
what he saw made him catch his breath.

She had blonde hair that fell past her shoulders in a long plait, and flawless skin. Her
legs were long and looked slim even in a
pair of white jeans. About five foot eight,
she was trim but athletic. She looked fit and
healthy, young and full of energy. Her blue
eyes sparkled, and he lost focus as he looked
into them. He was well aware that she was
the first woman he'd truly noticed in a long
time and for a brief moment Gemma was
not first and foremost in his mind.

And then the ever-present guilt resur-
faced.

Gemma was his responsibility. His burden to bear. This woman, Viktoria, was
gorgeous but their relationship was purely
professional. It didn't matter what she looked
like.

She was still smiling as he dug out his

army identification and passed it over. He waited while she inspected it and then showed it to her driver.

He stuck it back in his pocket when she returned it to him and resisted the urge to slam the passenger door when she finally climbed into his car. He might be frustrated but he still had the manners instilled into him not only from the army but from his parents and he remembered Doug's words. *'Be nice.'*

It shouldn't have been a hardship to spend the day with her and it wasn't her fault he was grumpy—that his guilt made him irritable.

He was mollified when his actions were rewarded with another smile.

'Merci.'

Her voice was pleasant. Deep for a woman. Her words precise. Her English was scattered with French words and slightly accented.

He resisted the temptation to ask her about it. He told himself he didn't need to know anything personal about her. That he didn't care to. He told himself he was just surprised. Working for the Prince, he'd expected her to be English, but he knew that would say more about him than her if he expressed his surprise. There was no reason why the Prince couldn't have anyone he liked working for him.

He'd keep the conversation generic, he decided as he started the engine. That was the safest option. 'I understand you want a tour of the facilities and competition venues for the Games?'

'Yes.'

'It's a bit of a drive to the old barracks which is where the majority of the events will be staged. Are you familiar with Sydney at all?'

'Not really. From what I have seen, though, it is a stunning city. And I have heard you have amazing beaches. I am looking forward to seeing Bondi Beach.'

'There are much better beaches to visit than Bondi.'

'Oh.'

He didn't think one tiny word could hold so much disappointment and he felt bad that he'd caused that. 'But you should still go there,' he said in an attempt to remedy the situation. He didn't need another thing to feel guilty about.

'I would really like to see the Outback and the Reef too. I want the full Australian experience.'

'You haven't been here before?'

'Never. I am very much looking forward to seeing your country.'

She sounded so eager and Cam couldn't decide if her enthusiasm was endearing or annoying. He couldn't remember the last time he'd been enthusiastic about anything. 'How long are you here for?'

'Fifteen days.'

'Including the Games?'

She nodded. *'Oui.'*

'You know it's a long way to anywhere in Australia, right? There's only so much you'll be able to see.'

'Yes.'

'Where are you from?'

'Berggrun.'

'Berggrun? Is that in Europe?' Cam had never heard of it, but he couldn't admit that. It was one thing for people to think you were ignorant, another to speak and confirm their suspicions and he did *not* want to appear a fool.

'You have heard of it?' she asked but he couldn't tell if she was surprised or pleased.

'No, I haven't,' he had to admit.

'It is in Europe.'

'It's a city?'

'No. A principality. A small one. It is only about the same size as Sydney.'

'Like Monaco?'

'Oui.'

'How did you get from there to working for Prince Alfred?'

'I have a degree in marketing.'

'That doesn't answer the question.'

'What question exactly?'

'The Prince's office asked me to show you around today. I just wondered what made you so important. Why you and no one else from his office?'

'No one else has arrived in Sydney yet. The Prince and everyone else with him are flying in via New Zealand in a couple of days.'

'Why didn't you come with them?'

'I do not normally work for the Prince. I am just working on this one event.'

He stopped his car at the entrance to the barracks and showed the guard their credentials before driving onto the grounds and, out of habit, parking near the medical centre.

He was going to ask her why she was working on this particular event, but she spoke again before he had a chance to.

'The hotel said you are a doctor,' Viktoria

said, looking around as he switched off the engine. 'Did they mean a medical doctor?'

'Of course.'

'Do you enjoy your job?'

He didn't really enjoy much any more but it kept him busy. He made a conscious effort to get through one day at a time. He'd been doing that for two years now, waiting for things to get better.

'It keeps me busy,' he replied.

He was a general surgeon but, when he wasn't deployed, he worked as a GP. He wouldn't be deployed again, he would not see active service again, but she didn't need to know any of that.

'If you are a doctor, why are you being my tour guide?'

That was a good question.

'A friend of mine is second-in-command for the Games and put me in charge of the medical team. I'm on the committee in addition to my day job,' he said as he headed around the medical centre towards the gym, hoping she would stop asking questions and follow his lead. 'This used to be an active army base but now it is a rehabilitation hospital and facility. The sports venues have been revamped and some additions have been made so that most of the events for the Legion's Games can be held here. What exactly is your brief?'

'I have to update the social media sites associated with the Games. I have to engage the competitors, tweet about the events and the results. I also want to promote the idea that physical and mental health have a link, but I am not sure just how I will do that yet.'

'What do you want to see?'

'Can I just wander around the facilities, get a feel for the space?'

'I don't have time to wander around the grounds with you.'

'If you can tell me if there is anywhere that is out of bounds for me, I am happy to wander on my own.'

Maybe he could do that— give her a quick overview and leave her to get on with it. That would give him some much-needed space; he was finding it difficult to concentrate with her around. He suspected she might be demanding but he could handle that; what he was concerned about was whether he could handle his own reaction to her. He was far too aware of her and it was making him edgy.

He was attracted to her and he didn't want to be.

'There's a medical facility and rehabilitation clinic on site. We have doctors, psychologists, physiotherapists, masseurs, exercise physiologists, podiatrists and prosthetists,' he said as he crossed the car park.

Viktoria matched his stride. She wasn't as tall as him but she moved quickly, her gait smooth and graceful. He wasn't as quick on his feet as he used to be, and he was concentrating hard to disguise his limp. He shouldn't care but he did. He didn't like to appear damaged.

He pushed open a door that led into the gym. There were basketball and volleyball courts overlooking a fifty-metre indoor pool with a traditional weights room and indoor rowing facility at the far end. It was an impressive facility.

'The sports are weightlifting, swimming, rowing, basketball, volleyball, cycling, archery and rugby?' She counted them off on her fingers. 'That is only eight. What have I missed?

'Tennis, athletics—track and field are counted separately—and sailing. Those events are not being held here, neither is the cycling, but the other seven events will be on this site. There's a rugby pitch and archery field outside.'

He walked with her along the pool deck

and into the gym. It was a hive of activity, with dozens of people in training. Some were competitors in the upcoming Games, others were taking part in rehabilitation programmes.

'Hey, Doc, do you have a minute?' one of the delisted vets called out as they walked past.

Cam stopped and introduced Viktoria to the soldier. 'Viktoria, this is Lieutenant Andrews.'

'Just Mark these days,' he said as he shook Viktoria's hand.

'Are you competing in the Games?' she asked.

He nodded. 'Archery and swimming.'

'Two sports?'

'Lots of us are doing multiple.'

'You have to get selected, yes? It is not a matter of simply turning up and putting your name on a list?' She turned to Cam with the question.

'That's correct. There are a thousand athletes registered from around the globe competing across a dozen different sports and most of the Aussies are competing in at least two sports, some three. The Games programme has been arranged to allow this. I haven't seen the final programme yet, but

I've heard it's massive. Most of the competitors have multiple events.'

'That was my plan too,' Mark said, 'but I'm getting a pain in my arm when I lift it above shoulder height. It's bad timing; it's affecting my aim in archery and also my stroke in the pool. Have you got time to take a look at it for me, Doc?'

'I'm consulting most of the day,' Cam said as he checked his watch. 'I'm due to start in twenty minutes. Head over to the clinic now and I'll make sure we squeeze you in.'

He turned back to Viktoria. He had work to do and he hadn't thought about the logistics of getting her back to the city. He should have let her driver bring her. 'Do you want to call your driver to collect you when you're done? I'll be busy for the next few hours.'

Her reply was unexpected. 'I am happy to stay. I can wander around until you are free. I can chat to the competitors if they are willing to talk to me. You have my cell phone number if you need to get hold of me.'

'I don't think I want you fraternising with the enemy,' he said, only half joking.

'I am not the enemy. I know there are medals on the line but Berggrun doesn't have any athletes in the Games and, even if we did, the Games are about more than competition. They are about mateship, camaraderie, a sense of belonging.'

'All right, I'll come and find you when I'm finished.' He couldn't be bothered arguing and he knew she was right. It irked him. *She* irked him. But it wasn't her confidence or even her tendency to challenge him that bothered him. It was simply the fact that he was aware of her.

His head was all over the place as he left her to go and tackle his consulting list. She was affecting his equilibrium, leaving him quite unsettled. He felt as though he'd been living in a haze, unaware of the world around him for two years and now, all of a sudden, he was noticing things. He was noticing her.

A pretty face and a foreign accent shouldn't be enough to make her interesting, but he knew he was kidding himself. He was intrigued but he wasn't willing to admit that he found her attractive. That he wanted to impress her.

She was calm, happy and relaxed. He was tense and grumpy. He had never thought that opposites did attract, and he couldn't speak for her but he was certainly attracted.

He focused on his patient list, squeezing

Mark into his diary, and tried not to think about Viktoria von Grasburg.

Several of the competitors had aches and pains from training, Mark included. Mark had been medically discharged from the army following a crippling leg injury and multiple surgeries. He was still battling depression but being chosen to compete in the Legion's Games had marked a big turning point in his recovery. Cam knew how important this competition was for him and he reluctantly gave him his diagnosis.

'I think you have sub-acromial bursitis,' he told him after conducting his assessment.

'What's that?'

'Inside the shoulder joint is a bursa, which is a small pouch filled with fluid that helps to reduce the friction of shoulder movements. That has become inflamed and swollen, which is affecting the quality of movement and causing your discomfort.'

'How did that happen?'

'It can present as a result of a fall, but it is most commonly an overuse injury, usually caused by repetitive overhead movements.'

'Like freestyle swimming.'

'Yes.'

'What do I do now?'

'Make an appointment with one of the physios.'

'What can they do?'

'A number of things: treatment, taping, exercises.'

'What about my events?'

'We'll know more once you've seen the physio. With your shoulder taped, archery might be possible; swimming might be more problematic, but don't write it off yet.'

'I'm sure I've heard about people having cortisone injections in their shoulders. Would that work?'

'Possibly, but if we went down that path I'd want you to rest your shoulder following the injection for a couple of weeks, which would mean you'd definitely miss your events. I'll organise an ultrasound scan just to be sure,' Cam said as he wrote a referral, 'but I'm pretty confident my diagnosis is accurate. Make an appointment to see the physio and we'll go from there.'

Cam finished his clinic and went in search of Viktoria. He found her in the gym, chatting to the athletes, just as she'd intimated. He stood inside the doorway for several minutes, observing her interaction with the competitors. It was obvious she had no shortage of people willing to talk to her.

That in itself was unusual. He knew from his own experience that many of the veterans were reluctant to talk to strangers. Many of them were physically or emotionally damaged, or both, and often that made them reticent to talk to people. Their scars went deep but they seemed perfectly happy to talk to Viktoria and she, in turn, seemed perfectly at ease talking to them. He was aware that she was able to draw people out. Or maybe she drew people in. He couldn't deny she had drawn him in.

She did seem very approachable. Despite her looks.

Maybe she was used to people giving her what she wanted, he thought. Beautiful people had a tendency to get away with things that ordinary people didn't.

With that slightly harsh thought, he left the shadows of the doorway and stepped into the gym. She noticed him approaching and smiled and Cam felt as if the sun had come out.

That reaction was unwanted, and he could feel grumpy Cam returning. The best thing he could do now was to drop her back to her hotel.

He needed time.

He needed space.

The smell of her perfume lingered in his car even after he'd dropped her back to her hotel—a floral scent, but not sweet. It was light, feminine, and enveloped him gently. It was pleasant, soothing.

His car suddenly felt too large for just one person. He was aware of a void, a feeling of emptiness.

That was ridiculous. He was used to being by himself. He'd spent a few hours with her; that wasn't long enough for her to make an impression. It shouldn't be long enough for him to notice her absence.

But a few hours in one day was more time than he'd spent with any stranger in the past year and more than he'd spent with many of his colleagues too. He could count on one hand the number of people he spent time with. Probably on three fingers—his sister, her husband and Doug. Not even his 'dates', for want of a better word, lasted more than a couple of hours. He'd become a bit of a recluse. Work, an occasional beer with colleagues, sporadic visits to his sister's farm and an even rarer date night were the sum total of his social activities. Even his exercise regime was solitary. He walked his dog and swam. Neither of which he did with company.

He didn't think he needed interaction with other people, he certainly didn't seek it out, yet he replayed snippets of the day, snatches of his conversation with Viktoria, as he drove home. He was surprised to find he remembered a lot of what she had said and even more about the way she spoke, the way she mixed her languages, the way she walked and smiled.

He let himself into his house, still thinking about Viktoria. That made a pleasant change to where his thoughts usually lay but he found it a little unsettling to be thinking so intently about a woman he'd just met.

He changed his clothes. He'd take his dog for a walk on the beach while he tried to clear his head.

The dog was a border collie, a retired farm dog, given to him by his sister. Skye had insisted that Cam take him when the dog was too old to work with the sheep any more. He wasn't a trained therapy dog, but his influence was the same. Cam always felt some of his stress dissolve when he walked Rex and today was no exception. Just the dog's company was enough to invoke calm; he had the same effect if they were just sitting still. Cam liked to keep one hand resting on Rex's head and that connection to another living, breathing being was always restorative.

He threw a ball for Rex—despite his age, the dog still wasn't truly happy unless he had a purpose—and let his mind wander as the dog ran up and down the small beach.

All his life, Cam had always had a plan. He'd always known what the next thing, the next five things, on his list of goals was. Where he was headed. He'd been certain of his path. Until two years ago.

What was the expression? *Man makes plans and God laughs.* Well, God had more than laughed at him. He'd given up on him altogether and Cam had struggled for the past two years. Since losing Gemma he'd felt rudderless.

The ache in his chest was gradually diminishing; emotionally and physically, he knew he was recovering, but it was a slow process. He knew he'd always hold Gemma in his heart but, even though the pain was no longer as acute, his future still looked bleak. There wasn't a lot he looked forward to. He was still just getting through one day at a time. As best he could. He'd forgotten what it was like to be excited about things.

Meeting Viktoria was possibly the most excited he'd felt about anything in a long time. He wasn't even excited about work. Work was a means to an end, but what end he wasn't sure. It was something to occupy his time.

Doug had tried to persuade him to compete in the Legion's Games. After all, the Games were for injured soldiers, those with both mental and physical wounds, and he knew he fell into both categories, but he'd resisted, hiding behind the apparent need for his services as a medic—using his job as an excuse to keep himself isolated.

He smiled wryly as he scratched behind his dog's ears and threw the ball again. He knew what he would say to any of his patients who were doing the same thing. He knew what he *had* said to them. But he was a firm believer in his patients doing as he said, not as he did. And he wasn't ready to let go of his pain just yet.

He was driven by guilt. Guilt was making him hold on to his pain as a punishment. He blamed himself for Gemma's death. He should have been able to save her.

He knew that if he hadn't been there that day, in the chopper when it went down, he would feel differently. If he hadn't been there the outcome would have been the same but that was different to being there and doing nothing. He knew in his head that she was dead before the chopper hit the ground. He knew there was nothing he could have done, but that didn't stop the guilt.

Survivor's guilt.

But giving it a name didn't make it any easier to live with. He would punish himself for a bit longer. He wasn't ready to let go of it just yet.

He had got used to the fact that Gemma was gone. That he was alone. He'd even got used to the idea that he would be alone for the rest of his life. But he hadn't got over the idea that all of it was somehow his fault.

He'd been through therapy—that had been non-negotiable under army guidelines— but he couldn't honestly say he felt any better for it. He knew all the statistics. He'd heard the spiel, read the research, but the fact of the matter was that nothing was going to make things return to the way they had been before the incident and he just had to get on with it, on with his life.

He was trying but he wasn't finding life very enthralling any more. The joy was gone.

Viktoria had arranged for Hendrik to drop her off at the base and she had spent the morning interviewing Games competitors. The base was busier today; veterans from other countries had arrived in Sydney and many of them were on site, utilising the training facilities ahead of the competition.

There was a lot of camaraderie between the competitors, which Viktoria had not been expecting. But, as they described their involvement, it became clearer. The veterans talked a lot about mateship and survival and the role the Games played in their recovery. While the Games were essentially a competition, Viktoria was realising they were about challenging yourself rather than beating others.

She wandered through the gym, past the stationary rowing machines where a solitary athlete was vigorously training. A Chocolate Labrador lay by her side and it was the dog that initially caught Viktoria's eye. As she got closer the woman's pace slowed.

Viktoria stopped beside the rower's right side and bent down, letting the dog sniff the back of her hand. 'What a gorgeous dog,' she said. 'What is his name?'

The athlete didn't acknowledge her, although the dog's ears pricked up. Viktoria hadn't meant to interrupt, she'd assumed she was finishing her regime, but perhaps she was doing interval training. Viktoria was about to apologise for interrupting and walk on when the athlete turned her head.

'Sorry, were you talking to me?' She pulled headphones out of her left ear as Viktoria spoke.

'Yes, I was just admiring your dog.'

'Would you mind standing on my left side?' the woman asked. Viktoria thought it was an odd request but moved around the machine as the woman explained, 'I've lost the vision in my right eye and I'm deaf in my right ear.'

'I asked what your dog is called.'

'This is Leroy—' the dog turned to look at the woman when he heard his name '—and I'm Fiona.'

'My name is Viktoria.'

'You don't look like you're defence force?' Fiona said as she slid her feet out of the straps and stood up.

Viktoria heard the question. Fiona was obviously curious about why Viktoria was there. 'I am not defence force, but I am working for Prince Alfred.'

'Doing what?'

'I am in charge of updating all the social media around the Games. Prince Alfred wants to keep the athletes connected but he also wants to promote the Games to the general public. He is keen to raise awareness of mental health and the benefits of exercise.'

'I can vouch for the benefits of exercise,' Fiona said as she scratched behind Leroy's ears. 'Exercise and my four-legged mate have made all the difference to me.'

'Is Leroy a guide dog?' Now that Fiona was standing, Viktoria was well aware that she had lost the sight in her right eye.

'Not exactly. He has multiple hats to wear. Technically, he is a service dog and he will assist me with my hearing and vision issues, but he's really been trained as a therapy animal. He does help me when I'm out or when someone stands on the wrong side of me. I had no idea you were there until his ears pricked up, then I knew to look out for something.'

'He is a therapy dog?'

'Yes. I sustained a head injury and lost the sight in one eye and the hearing in one ear on a tour of duty when a roadside bomb exploded under a vehicle I was travelling in, but the thing Leroy helps most with is managing my PTSD. Since the incident I struggle in traffic, big crowds, unfamiliar environments. Leroy helps calm me down.'

'But you are competing in the Games?'

Viktoria asked. Sweat was dripping off Fiona; she certainly looked as though she'd been training hard. 'The organisers are expecting large crowds. Is that going to be a problem for you?' Viktoria wondered how Fiona would cope with the crowds and the noise that would come with them.

Fiona nodded. 'I am competing but only in the stationary rowing. That's a controlled environment. Indoors. Only a certain number of people competing, limited by the number of machines. And it's not going to be quite such a popular spectator sport as, say, the basketball or swimming. Fewer spectators, less noise. And Leroy can stay beside me. He couldn't do that in most of the other events.'

'He really helps?'

'Definitely. I don't leave the house without him.'

As Viktoria spoke to Fiona she thought about the tales other athletes had already recounted to her and the role she could play took shape in her mind. There was a bigger story to be told. She could do much more than post pictures on social media. She would write brief articles on the competitors—delve into their stories if they would let her, take their stories to the world. She would use the

Games to highlight not only the benefits of exercise but to show what these competitors from all over the globe had in common. Some of the athletes had physical disabilities, others emotional, but they all carried scars and it was those scars that united them. She would showcase their resilience, their mateship and their determination and maybe inspire others through those stories.

She wandered through the gym and out onto the pool deck as she thought about how to get the ball rolling. She wondered if she could ask Cam for help. He hadn't made any plans to meet her today and she had no idea if he was even on the base, but she kept one eye out for him anyway.

As she walked beside the pool, she spied Mark, the ex-soldier she had met yesterday, sitting on the edge. He looked up as she approached and smiled in recognition.

She stopped to say hello. 'Have you been swimming? I thought you were injured?'

'I have a sore shoulder.' He shrugged. 'I've had worse injuries.'

Mark was heavily tattooed across his back and arms but sports tape over his shoulder partially obscured some of the tattoos.

He pushed himself up out of the water to stand on the edge of the pool and Viktoria noticed that his left leg had been amputated below the knee. She hadn't realised yesterday.

He hopped easily over to a chair on the pool deck, where he sat to towel himself dry. A prosthetic leg stood beside the chair.

Viktoria followed him. 'I thought you said swimming aggravated your shoulder?'

'Yes, it does. But until someone tells me I have to stop I'm going to keep swimming. I guess I don't like being told I can't do something,' he said as he slid his prosthesis on.

'And Dr Hamilton did not tell you to stop?'

'No. He sent me to get some scans done of my shoulder, which showed I have an inflamed bursa, and he sent me to the physiotherapist. I'm going back to see her shortly for more treatment.' Mark pulled a pair of trackpants over his bathers and stood up. 'What are you doing here?'

'I came to take some photographs, but I have been talking to some of the competitors and now I am looking for stories.'

'Stories?'

'I want to tell the stories of the competitors. Do you think people would be willing to talk to me?'

'About what?'

'I want to acknowledge the struggles and the sacrifices you have all made. I know not everyone will want to tell their stories publicly, but I'm sure, out of a thousand competitors, some will. What do you think? Could I interview you?'

He hesitated. She could see his deliberation. 'Me?'

She nodded. 'Prince Alfred is keen to showcase the benefits of exercise in promoting recovery, both physical and mental, and I think this is a way we could do that. Will you help me? Can we at least give it a try?'

'I'll think about it.'

Viktoria spent the rest of the afternoon talking to various athletes before making her way to the medical centre. She had dropped in there earlier and asked for a time to catch up with Cam. She hadn't heard from him at all and, after speaking with Freddie about her idea, she wanted Cam's opinion.

'Hello, Viktoria.' Cam stood up as she entered his office. 'What can I do for you?'

'I need your opinion.'

'You didn't need to make an appointment to see me for that,' he said as he repositioned a chair for her.

'I had not heard from you today,' she re-

plied with a shrug, 'and I did not know if
I would see you…so…' She sat and Cam
perched on the edge of his desk. 'I saw Mark
today when I was at the pool. He'd been
swimming. I wondered why, when he is injured, you did not tell him to stop.'

'That's what you wanted to see me about?'

'Not only that, but it is related in a way.'

'I can't discuss Mark with you.'

Cam stood and moved around the desk to
sit in his chair and Viktoria wasn't sure if
he was distancing himself from her or just
her line of questioning. She rephrased her
question.

'I am not asking you to discuss his injury —he has already explained the problem
to me—I am simply asking you to explain
why you did not stop him from training.'

'Because it was highly unlikely that he
would listen. These men and women who
have seen active service aren't likely to let
someone like me, or something like this —
a relatively minor injury —stop them. It's
about managing the problem, not dictating
to them what they can and can't do. They're
used to taking orders in their job; it's important to give them some control of their
bodies.'

Viktoria could respect their need to have some control. She felt the same way.

'Mark is intelligent enough to make his own decisions,' Cam continued. 'You'll see. He's swimming in a relay—if he doesn't pull up well enough I'm sure he'll make the right decision for the team. If there's one thing most soldiers are good at it is being part of a team. But tell me, how is that related to your other question?'

'After speaking to many of the competitors today I also spoke with Prince Alfred and we think that it would be good to do some articles on what soldiers go through emotionally and what families or loved ones can do to support them. Obviously, getting back into physical exercise is a great outcome for a lot of people but it is a challenge for so many. There must be a lot of stress on everyone, the families and the soldiers, when they are dealing with these issues. I wanted to link the benefits of exercise to positive mental health and Prince Alfred and I think this could be a good way to do that. Your insight would be really useful. Would you be prepared to talk to me about your views?'

'My views?'

'*Oui.*'

'On what?'

'To get a professional perspective on what the athletes have gone through.'

She'd noticed his limp and wondered if he had his own personal story to tell but she suspected he wouldn't be very forthcoming. He asked questions of her but had given her nothing personal. She thought she was a master of being able to make conversation with all types of people, but she struggled to get anything much out of Dr Campbell Hamilton. Perhaps a professional opinion piece would build some trust and, if nothing else, she was sure it would be interesting.

'I can't give you any specifics about the athletes and I really don't have the time.'

She had hoped he would agree. It would be a way to spend a bit more time with him. She was attracted to him. He was sexy in a brooding, distant way and she wanted him to like her. She was used to people being excited to meet her, being keen for her attention, but he seemed as if he just wanted to be left alone. If he wasn't so sexy, she'd be inclined to do just that but she was very aware of him and she wanted to get to know him better.

She definitely had a type and Cam fitted into that perfectly. She had always been attracted to tall, dark and handsome men but usually they were charming too. Cam was an enigma. His manners were impeccable, but he seemed to be operating on autopilot.

He was a challenge.

And she was definitely up for the challenge.

'It would not take a lot of time.'

She waited for him to relent but he said nothing. The silence stretched between them.

'Would you think about it?' she asked with a smile. 'You have to admit it would be a good way to raise awareness of the issues surrounding mental health.'

'Do you think you can simply smile at me and get your own way? Hasn't anyone ever said no to you before?'

'Not often,' she admitted. She wasn't used to being told no. She was used to people doing what she asked. She supposed it was one of the perks of being a princess, but it looked as if she had her work cut out for her trying to get favours from Cam. 'Please, think about it. I am happy to go over any concerns you might have. We can discuss it over dinner?'

'Dinner?'

She nodded. 'I am free tonight.'

'Tonight?'

'Yes. Are you busy?' Nothing ventured, nothing gained, she figured.

Yes, he was busy.

'I'm going for a swim,' he said, perhaps a little too abruptly. His leg was aching, and he knew he needed to exercise to loosen up his hip. He also needed to exercise to clear his head.

He had known Viktoria was on the base today, but he'd deliberately steered clear of her. Even so, she had crept into his thoughts on numerous occasions, making it hard to concentrate on his work. It was a slightly infuriating situation. He liked feeling in control and he was definitely thrown by her. He didn't like feeling off-kilter.

'Are you swimming for exercise or therapy?'

'Pardon?'

'I have seen you limping. You are injured, *non*?'

He hadn't disguised his limp as well as he'd hoped but his limp was none of her business. The rebuke was on the tip of his tongue, but she apologised before he could say anything, defusing his temper.

'No matter. You cannot swim all night,

surely?' she asked. 'Shall we meet afterwards?'

Not everyone wants to talk to you.

He bit back another terse reply, knowing it was his own guilt that was making him unsettled. His bad mood was not her fault.

He hadn't wanted her to see his weakness.

He wanted to make a good impression on her and knowing that annoyed him. He hadn't cared about impressing anyone for a long time. He had kept his feelings locked away—he didn't want to share them; he didn't want to let anyone in—and he wasn't about to share his feelings with her. But he also didn't want to appear rude.

He was going to make up an excuse, but he didn't want to lie to her. She hadn't done anything to deserve that.

'Or I could come with you,' she said.

She was persistent. He'd give her that.

He didn't mind a determined personality unless it made his life difficult, and he suspected she would make his life difficult. Not in the sense that she would complain about his behaviour but in the sense that she would complicate his life.

She was obviously used to getting her own way. It should annoy him, but he knew he wanted to give in to her too. But his stubborn streak made it hard to give in gracefully.

After his swim he was supposed to be going to a fundraising function for Doug's cricket club. He'd bought his ticket as a favour to Doug but he'd never intended to go, but somehow the night had arrived and he hadn't begged off yet. He was about to put her off when he realised that she would give him the perfect excuse to get out of attending the fundraiser. He knew Doug had invited him partly to get him out socialising, but he also knew Doug would cut him some slack if he said he had a date. Maybe he was stretching the truth and the friendship, but he'd text Doug anyway—he would never know. He would make sure he gave a big donation instead. He was sure he wouldn't be missed.

So, instead of making his excuses to Viktoria he said, 'Do you have a pair of swimmers with you?'

'*Non.*'

'Are you planning on skinny-dipping then?' If he closed his eyes he knew he'd be able to picture her naked. He shouldn't be able to, but he knew her features were imprinted on his brain already.

'*Quoi? Non!* Where are you swimming?

I can buy a swimsuit or you could lend me a T-shirt.'

That conjured up a whole other image, of Viktoria in one of his T-shirts, wet and clinging to her curves.

He fought the urge to close his eyes and said, 'I was planning on swimming at home. Would you like to come with me?' He spoke without thinking, without stopping to consider the consequences.

She smiled in reply and he knew he was in trouble.

She was beautiful, smart and she radiated warmth. The trifecta. And he was fascinated, intrigued, unsettled.

He was in big trouble.

CHAPTER THREE

WHAT WAS HE THINKING?

He wasn't sure. He wasn't thinking clearly, that much was certain. He was unsettled. Viktoria was disturbing his equilibrium and now she was about to step inside his house.

What the hell was he doing?

He didn't know that either.

He actually hadn't thought she would take him up on his offer but when she had nodded and smiled widely he hadn't regretted the invitation.

He hadn't brought a woman home in two years and he'd never brought a woman to this house. Gemma hadn't even seen this house. He'd bought it after the incident, when he'd needed a single storey house with easy access. The pool was a bonus. The privacy even more so.

The only female who had visited him here was his sister. And now Viktoria.

Was he making a mistake?

It was too late now, he thought as he unlocked his front door. The offer had been extended and accepted.

He tried not to feel as if he was cheating on Gemma. Tried to convince himself that the invitation he'd extended to Viktoria was completely innocent, devoid of any attraction. But he knew that wasn't the case.

But that didn't mean he was going to act on his feelings. For all he knew Viktoria had no interest in him. Why would she? He was certain she would have her pick of men. Why would she look twice at him?

He was kidding himself, thinking he was in control of the situation because he had issued the invitation. He knew, very clearly, that she was in charge and he suspected he had just become one in a long line of men who hadn't been able to refuse her requests. Another who had succumbed to her wishes because of an innate need to please her, to see her smile, to feel enveloped in her warmth.

He pushed open the door and held it for Viktoria to enter first, but her way was blocked by a very excited Border collie with a rapidly wagging tail.

'*Bonjour.* What is your name?' Viktoria

asked as she bent over and offered the back of her hand for the dog to sniff before rubbing his head.

Cam was treated to a delightful and distracting view of Viktoria's backside as she bent over in front of him. He did his best not to stare, focusing on his dog instead. 'This is Rex and it looks like he's expecting a walk.' He gave two short, low whistles followed by a slightly longer one and Rex left Viktoria and came to his side, allowing Viktoria space to enter his house. She took three steps and came to a halt again as her attention was captured by the view.

'Oh! Très magnifique!'

To their right a passage led away to the bedrooms but in front of them the entry hall opened up into a large open-plan kitchen and living space. An expanse of windows stretched across the far wall, making the room seem part of the outdoors. Through the windows the eye was drawn over the infinity pool to the ocean beyond and Cam knew that was what had caught Viktoria's eye. The view was incredible.

His house was stunning, simple and modern with clean lines, but it was the view that captured one's attention. The house was perched on the edge of a cliff overlooking a small private beach which only a handful of houses had access to and the view and the seclusion were the reasons Cam had chosen this property over the other single-level houses he had inspected. He had sunk his inheritance and his compensation from the incident into this house, but it had been worth every dollar.

He'd bought it eighteen months ago. After the incident. Gemma had never seen this house and that was how he liked it. There were no memories here.

The views over the ocean were stunning but the house itself was a clean slate, a blank canvas. Somewhere he could escape to. Somewhere he could forget about the past. Somewhere he could have solitude.

The furnishings were sparse and there were very few personal effects but that didn't bother him; it was the view that captured the attention and furnishings and artwork were never going to be able to compete. It appeared as if the furnishings had been kept deliberately minimalistic but the reality was he had never bothered to furnish it properly. He never entertained and the only visitors were his sister, her husband and Doug.

Rex was weaving circles around his legs and Cam decided that a walk would be a better form of exercise given the circumstances. He didn't trust himself to take Viktoria swimming in one of his old shirts. A walk seemed like the safer option.

He changed out of his army fatigues into a T-shirt and a pair of shorts, long enough to almost cover the scar that ran down the outside of his right thigh. He could just make out the end of it at the edge of his knee but if he walked on Viktoria's right side he didn't think she would notice the mark. He left his feet bare and led her down the wooden steps that led to the beach.

'This is so pretty,' she said as they made their way down to the sand.

The beach was small, only a hundred metres from end to end, curved between two cliffs. The sand was golden and fine, and the water was crystal-clear. For now, they had it to themselves. A little piece of paradise and tranquillity.

He threw the ball for Rex as Viktoria slipped off her shoes. She held her arms out wide and tipped her face up to the sun as she twirled in circles. She was like a bubble of sunshine, a balloon of happiness floating along the beach. If she had a string Cam felt he could grab hold of her and absorb some of her positive energy.

'Are you always this upbeat?' he asked.

She wobbled slightly as she stopped twirling. 'It is impossible not to enjoy this,' she said with a smile. 'It is a beautiful day in a beautiful place. I feel free. Like I am on holiday, far from everything.'

'You mentioned you're only working for Prince Alfred for these games. What do you do for work at home?' Cam asked as he bent down to retrieve Rex's ball.

'I am involved in events.'

'What sort of events?'

'Polo matches, charities, galas.'

'In Berggrun?'

'Yes.'

'Does your population support all those events?'

'We are a tourist hot spot and in Europe there are constantly events. It is not far for people to hop from one country to another if there is an event worth attending.'

They walked the length of the sand while Rex chased the ball until he started to tire. As they turned at the far end of the beach Viktoria stopped and rolled up the bottoms of her wide-leg navy linen trousers and waded into the water. Rex barked and dashed in after her, gently pushing against the backs of her calves, which Cam had to admit were rather shapely, until Viktoria found herself out of the water again.

She was laughing as Rex herded her back to Cam. 'What is he doing?'

'He's rounding you up. Bringing you into line,' Cam said with a smile. He was surprised to feel a smile on his face; he couldn't remember the last time he had smiled spontaneously, the last time he'd felt happy. Viktoria was making him feel things he didn't expect. Her happiness and her delight in the day was rubbing off on him.

'Why?'

'It's in his nature. He's a sheepdog.'

'Why do you have a sheepdog?'

'He's retired, or supposed to be, but it seems he hasn't got the memo yet. He belonged to my sister, but when she retired him she thought he should come and live with me. That was kinder than trying to keep him out of the paddocks,' he told her as Rex proceeded to shake the water from his fur and showered them with the droplets.

Cam hadn't wanted to take responsibility for a dog, but Skye had insisted. Tired of his stubbornness and his refusal to agree to her suggestion, she had arrived on his doorstep one day with the dog in tow, and left him with Cam.

That had been a year ago. Cam had still been on medical leave from the defence force and the days had stretched endlessly before him. With no real reason to get out of bed, it had been all too easy to let the days blur together. Skye had insisted that having a dog would motivate him to get up and she'd been right. Having Rex around had made Cam get out of bed but, even better, the dog was company. He listened without judgement, and hadn't minded Cam's tears, and lay by his side when he cried.

'Are you going to swim?' Viktoria's question brought Cam back to the present.

'I don't think I need to now.' His leg had loosened up with the walk and he didn't want to swim alone. He assumed she wasn't about to join him without bathers. He would swim in his pool later if he needed to.

Viktoria tucked her hand into the crook of his elbow as she walked beside him.

He let himself relax into the moment and it actually felt good to let his thoughts go.

He knew he was wound tight, but he found it hard to take a deep breath, he found it hard to relax. He knew he tended to keep busy, sometimes frantically so, as that didn't give him time to dwell on the past or think about a future that was different to how he'd imagined. But to actually just stop and be in the moment, in the present, was okay. He didn't need to think about the past or the future. He could just be.

Their steps were in sync and left two sets of perfect footprints in the damp sand. Confirmation that he had shared this moment with her. A moment he didn't regret.

'Thank you for bringing me here,' she said. 'It has been a much nicer way to spend the evening than being in my hotel.'

He felt a little guilty that he'd only invited her to join him as it had given him an excuse to get out of Doug's function.

The sun was low in the sky by the time they climbed the steps back to the house. 'Would you like to go out for dinner?' she asked. 'My treat, in return though I want to pick your brains about the issues facing the athletes.'

'I can throw something on the barbecue,' he said. He was reluctant to go out; he was enjoying her company and he wanted that feeling to last a little longer. If they went out, other people would intrude on their space and he selfishly wanted to keep her to himself.

* * *

Viktoria couldn't cook—she'd never needed to learn—but she chopped vegetables for the salad while Cam barbecued lamb fillets.

They ate on the terrace overlooking the ocean and the sparkling lights of the other houses on the clifftops. Their conversation flowed smoothly, and Viktoria was able to get Cam's opinion on what she had discussed with the athletes. She had spoken to several of the Games competitors and they all had similar stories to tell. How the commitment to an exercise regime had helped to get them out of bed or socialising again. How exercise and the Games had given them a focus. How the feeling of pushing themselves, of setting and achieving goals, had given them a purpose. In short, how exercise had saved them.

Their conversation alternated between the Games and her life in Berggrun, but it wasn't until Cam had cleared their plates that she realised he'd given her very little insight into his own life. While he did answer some of her questions about army life, his answers were generic, giving her no insight into his personal experiences. Even his house gave no hints as to his life and the type of man he was. There were no family photographs; he'd mentioned a sister but there was no sign of her, nor was there any sign of parents or friends. No holiday snaps. No hobbies.

She would have liked to have tried again to steer the conversation back to him, but she was aware it was getting late and she still had work to do.

'Thank you for dinner. I should call Hendrik to collect me.' They had shared a bottle of wine and Viktoria assumed Cam wouldn't want to drive her home and nor did she expect him to.

'Why do you have a driver?' he asked.

She had always had a driver and didn't actually have a driver's licence. She had never had the need for one, but she knew telling him that would invite a lot more questions. 'Because we drive on the opposite side of the road in Berggrun and we thought it was safer not to drive here.'

'We do have taxis, you know.'

She would never be allowed in a taxi. Especially not unaccompanied. 'Hendrik won't mind; he'll be expecting me to call. What is your address?'

Cam told her his address and then went out onto the terrace to bring in their glasses, giving her some privacy.

'*Bonjour*, Hendrik,' Viktoria said when he

answered. 'Are you able to collect me from Vaucluse? I have the address.'

'*Oui*, Your Highness, I know where you are.'

'*Comment?*'

'It is my job. I did a search on the doctor.'

'*Quoi? Pourquoi?*'

'I run a check on anyone you are alone with. I was not about to risk my job by leaving you unprotected. I am outside already.'

She should be cross. She was not even allowed that little bit of freedom. But she couldn't mind because she'd had a wonderful night. And Hendrik was right—it was his job; she couldn't argue or berate him for doing his job.

'How long did it take you to get here?'

'Twenty minutes.'

'I will meet you outside in twenty minutes.' She would delay leaving, partly because she didn't want to go, although she knew she had to, but mainly because she didn't want Cam to wonder how Hendrik had arrived so quickly.

'*D'accord. Vingt minutes.*'

She kissed Cam on both cheeks and thanked him again as he walked her outside to where Hendrik waited.

Hendrik held the door for her and she slid into the back seat, wishing she could have given Cam a proper kiss goodnight, but she couldn't do that in front of her bodyguard. Even if she was denying her royal background there were still rules that needed to be followed.

'Hendrik, will you be shadowing me all the time?' she asked as he pulled the car away from the kerb.

'*Oui*, Your Highness,' came his reply.

'Even when I'm with Dr Hamilton?'

'Always.'

That was not part of her newly formed plan.

Coming to Sydney had been her chance to have one last adventure. She hadn't expected to meet a man like Campbell Hamilton. She still hadn't been able to shake the feeling that they had been destined to meet. That there was a reason he had been sent to collect her, that a higher power was at work. She hadn't intended to have one last fling but if the opportunity presented itself with Cam she wanted to take advantage of it and, to do that, she needed to find a way of getting away from Hendrik's protective observation. 'Do you think, if he's trusted by the Australian government as part of their armed forces, you could trust him too?'

'He is not part of *our* armed forces.'

'We don't have an armed force. We have palace guards.'

'Well, he is not a Berggruner.'

'I understand, but you said you did a search on him. Did you find anything suspicious about him?'

'Non.'

'What *did* you find?'

She was curious. She wished she'd asked Cam more questions but perhaps Hendrik could shed some light on him.

'He is thirty-four years old. He was raised on a sheep station and has served in the army for four years. He has done two tours of Afghanistan and was injured during his last deployment.'

Viktoria knew Campbell carried an injury of some sort—she had noticed his limp—but he hadn't mentioned it. She wondered if Hendrik would tell her. She wondered if she should wait to see if Cam would. But she knew she didn't want to wait. She wanted to know as much about him as she could. 'Do you know what happened?'

'He was in a helicopter that was shot down. Everyone else on board was killed.

He almost didn't make it. He sustained a collapsed lung, fractured ribs, leg and pelvis, and a ruptured spleen.'

'How long ago was this?'

'Two years.'

She wanted to know who was with him. Who'd nursed him back to health. Who was there for his recovery. Where was his family?

But she couldn't ask Hendrik any of that. It wouldn't do to show that much interest. As far as Hendrik was concerned her relationship with Cam was strictly professional.

Cam swam one final lap of the pool before he hauled himself out, towelled off and padded inside. He had needed to swim after all, not to ease his muscles but to cool down. He had enjoyed the evening far more than he'd expected and it had left him energised and buoyant. He'd needed to burn off some of that energy before he'd be able to sleep.

He flicked on the light as he stepped into his bedroom and the one personal photo displayed in the house caught his eye.

On his bedside table was a photo of him with Gemma.

A familiar pang of guilt flared through him as he looked at her smiling face.

He turned his back on the photo and went to hang his towel in the en-suite bathroom.

The evening had been perfectly innocent, but he still felt as if he was cheating on Gemma. The few dates he had been on in the past twelve months hadn't gone past a drink or dinner and the occasional kiss. He'd always held back, unwilling to expose his scars, emotional and physical, and unwilling to cheat on Gemma. The evening with Viktoria had been more innocent than some but he still felt guilty and this time he knew it was because he wanted to see her again. This time he wasn't done. This time he didn't want to say goodbye.

He knew it was time he moved on—he knew he shouldn't feel guilty about enjoying himself—but the guilt had become part of him and letting it go was hard.

He stepped out of the bathroom and looked again at the photograph, at Gemma's wide smile. He could almost hear her voice and he knew what she would say.

She would tell him to get on with his life.

She had never stopped. She'd always had a purpose, just as he always had a goal. He knew Gemma would not want him to stagnate, but that still wasn't enough to assuage his guilty conscience. He knew his world had become insular, that work and exercise were his only focus and that it wasn't healthy. He knew he needed to spend time with other people, that he was at risk of becoming a recluse, but he hadn't been very good company recently.

But maybe he could start with a small step outside his insular world. Maybe it was time.

He went over to the photo and laid it face down. He didn't want to put it away, not yet, but he found he didn't want to look at it any more tonight. Tonight, he was going to go to sleep with thoughts of Viktoria in his head.

Viktoria thanked the hotel chauffeur and hurried across the army base. She was running late after an early morning drama. Hendrik's wife and child had been involved in a car accident in Berggrun. His wife had sustained a fractured elbow and ribs and Hendrik had flown home to be with them, leaving Viktoria and Brigitta in Sydney. Viktoria didn't mind; the hotel had chauffeurs available and she knew this would give her more freedom. In her opinion that was a good thing.

She smiled as she headed for the mess hall. She was still thinking about the feel of Cam's cheek under her lips as she'd kissed him goodbye last night. Thinking about the taste of the sea on his skin and the smell of the sun in his hair.

She'd enjoyed the evening. Even if he hadn't opened up to her, he had relaxed. He'd seemed calmer in his own domain. Whether it was the glass of wine, the walk on the beach, the familiar environment or the company of his dog she wasn't sure, but she'd liked that side of him.

His house had surprised her, though. It was stunning but it hadn't felt like a home. She hadn't had a lot of experiences with regular houses, but she had expected to feel a sense of Cam within the walls. She'd expected to see something of the man he was, even if it was just a glimpse, but she'd been able to glean very little about him. It made her wonder why he was so guarded. What was he hiding?

She had no idea but at least she hadn't seen any evidence of a woman in his life and for that she was grateful. She'd been made a fool of once before and, even if she was only hoping for a fling, she didn't want to make a mistake. She'd been a poor judge of character in the past but, while she knew there was something Cam wasn't telling her, probably a great many things, she was confident that he wasn't hiding a girlfriend or a wife.

Only the dog seemed to have some personal meaning for Cam.

It felt as if only Rex tied Cam to the house, and he had been a gift from Cam's sister. Cam hadn't chosen the dog, but he had kept him and he was obviously fond of him. That had pleased her—someone who was able to form a bond with an animal had to have a kind heart, she thought as she arrived at the mess hall.

She had made arrangements to meet Lieutenant Andrews on the base this morning to begin their interview and he was waiting for her in front of the mess hall. '*Bonjour*, Mark. How are you today?'

'I'm good. Have you eaten? I thought we could grab some breakfast while we chat.'

Viktoria didn't eat breakfast—black coffee was her morning go-to—but she thought Mark might find it easier to talk if the focus was on a meal instead of directly on him. 'I do not need breakfast, but I will have a coffee,' she replied as he held the door open for her to enter the mess hall. 'How is your shoulder today?'

'The physio has told me I need to rest it from swimming,' he said as he picked up a tray and joined the queue for food. 'But I can do light exercises in the gym.'

Viktoria stood beside him as he chose his food. It didn't look particularly appetising and she was glad she didn't eat breakfast. 'What about your archery? Are you able to continue with that?'

'Yes. That's uncomfortable but the physio doesn't think I'll do any more damage.'

'Have you always done these sports?' she asked as they sat down at a table.

'No. I could swim, most Aussie kids can, but I've never swum competitively so that's new for me.'

'Which do you enjoy more?'

'Archery helps with my mental focus and balance. But, while I thought I'd like the solitary style of archery, I'm finding I enjoy swimming more. I'm swimming one individual event and also a relay and I like feeling like part of a team again. After my injury I really missed that. Comradeship is such a big part of army life and it's good to feel that again.'

'How long have you been in the army?'

'I joined straight out of school and that was twenty years ago. My dad and my grandpa both served.'

'When did you get injured?'

'Three years ago.'

'What happened?' She felt bad for asking, suddenly it felt very intrusive, but Mark had agreed to be interviewed and he knew the reason behind her quest for the stories.

'I was actually injured in a training exercise. I got tangled in a parachute and broke a lot of bones. My leg was so badly busted that even after multiple surgeries I was in constant pain. I decided in the end to have it amputated. It seemed like the best solution. And it helped. Physically I improved but mentally I was still a mess. I was angry. With the army, myself, my wife. It took me a long time to sort myself out and my marriage broke down.'

'I am sorry to hear that.'

'It happens a lot. The families put up with a lot, getting moved around every three years, having us deployed overseas, not knowing if we'll come back. It's stressful. And then we come back and we're not the same any more. Even if we haven't got physical injuries, we've got emotional scars. We've seen things no one should see. Sometimes we've also done things no one should have to do and that leaves a mark, you know? And it's not something we can talk about to anyone who hasn't been there. No one would understand. So, after everything my wife and I went through over the years, my injury was the last straw. And it wasn't even the injury. It was the black hole of depression that I fell into that finished us off.

'And then I had nothing. No marriage. No career. I was lost without my wife, without the army, without my mates. It's been a long road back. The Games have brought me back and now, here I am.'

'What made you want to compete in the Games?'

'One of my mates took part in the last Games and he convinced me to have a go at competing in this one. Having to get out of bed to exercise really was my salvation.'

Viktoria had initially thought Mark seemed to have his life together and it surprised her to hear the level of despair that was evident in his voice. She hoped she could do his story justice.

She reminded herself that Mark and soldiers like him were the reason Freddie had started the Games. His story, while difficult to listen to, could help others who found themselves in the same predicament he had.

Mark's next words reinforced her sentiments. 'If each one of us who has been through something like this can help one other person then the cumulative effect could be enormous. Each person who finds the strength and the will to get out of bed in the morning and face another day is a triumph. I wasn't ever suicidal but some of my mates have been. That's why these Games are so important. They have given so many of us a purpose, a goal, something to aim for. I just hope I get to be a part of it.'

'You will be a part of it even if you cannot compete but what will happen if you cannot swim the relay because of your shoulder?' Would he be letting others down? What would the knock-on effect of that be? she wondered.

'We can substitute another athlete if necessary but I'm really hoping I can swim the relay—that will be my highlight, I suspect—but I guess time will tell. I'm going to continue with the modified exercises that the physio has given me. I'm heading over to the gym now to do a light cardio session with the rest of my relay team and we're having dinner together tonight. You should meet the team; they might be happy to do interviews for you too,' he said as he pushed the last bit of his scrambled eggs onto a corner of toast and finished it off. 'Why don't you come to dinner with us?'

'I would not want to intrude,' Viktoria replied as she recalled Cam's comment about being the enemy.

'You wouldn't be intruding—our wives and girlfriends are coming too; you're more than welcome. You might like to meet some of the families—they got us through the tough times.'

He was right. She had no other plans for the evening, and it would be interesting to meet the athletes' support network. *'D'accord,'* she accepted. 'That sounds good.'

Viktoria stepped into the pub and immediately saw Mark seated at a large table in the far corner. She joined the group and made sure to concentrate as Mark introduced her to his teammates. They had all suffered injuries in active service although Bud had also sustained several sporting injuries playing rugby which had also taken a toll. He was suffering from PTSD following multiple surgeries on his back, ankles and knee. Sean had a back injury and Eric had bilateral lower leg amputations.

Despite their injuries, Viktoria found them to have a positive outlook, although they made it clear that hadn't always been the case and it had been a long road for them all to get to this point.

She listened as they explained how the Legion's Games had given them all a focus but, more importantly, brought them together again. They all expressed that they had experienced a sense of isolation due to their injuries and that they missed the camaraderie of belonging to a team. It was clear that their defence force family was important to them. For Bud, in particular, it was his only family.

Sean's wife, Lisa, recounted how difficult things had been when Sean injured his back. She had been pregnant at the time and not only had Sean been unable to help physically when she was heavily pregnant, but he'd also been unable to pick up their baby when she was born. His pain had made him miserable and the whole experience of becoming parents had been marred by his moods. It had put a strain on their marriage, but they had got through that and were now expecting a second child. As Lisa was saying how she hoped they would be able to enjoy the next experience, Viktoria's gaze was drawn across the room. She couldn't have said what made her turn in that direction at that point in time, perhaps a sixth sense of some sort, because her gaze landed on Cam. She'd had no idea he was joining them and perhaps he was also unaware of her presence as she saw his slight double-take when he noticed her sitting with the group.

He greeted everyone and slid in to sit on the bench seat beside her, which was the only empty place. His thigh brushed against hers, just briefly as he sat down, and she could feel the heat of his body through the thin fabric of her skirt triggering a flurry of nerves.

'Hello, Viktoria. I didn't know you were going to be here.'

She hoped her presence didn't bother him. She thought seeing him was a pleasant surprise, but she almost felt as if she should be apologising. 'Mark invited me. He thought I would like to meet some of the families. He did not tell me you were coming.'

'I catch up with the boys when I can. I served in Afghanistan with Sean and Bud,' he said as he poured himself a drink from the jug of beer that Mark passed to him.

Viktoria sipped her wine and tried not to think about Cam sitting beside her. About the way his leg brushed against hers each time he gestured in conversation. His touch, even a brief graze, was enough to trigger a powerful reaction. Her heart rate accelerated and her breathing quickened. She had never experienced an effect like this before.

The talk moved on from their time in the army to tales of cricket, rugby and children.

'Do you have children, Viktoria?' Lisa asked.

'*Non.*' Viktoria shook her head.

'She's much too busy working for the Prince,' Cam said.

'The Prince? As in Prince Alfred?' Lisa asked, the excitement evident in her voice.

'*Oui.*'

'Do you think we could meet him?'

Viktoria was surprised. 'You want to meet him? I did not think you Australians cared about the Royal Family too much.'

'You're probably right—' Sean began, before Lisa nudged him and interrupted.

'It's not about meeting royalty—it's about meeting the man who started these Games.'

'If it wasn't for him, none of us would be here today; it's quite likely none of us would have our men in our lives still,' Eric's wife added.

'We'd like to thank him,' Lisa said.

'I will see what I can do,' Viktoria told them, thinking Freddie would be pleased to hear from the wives. 'He will be at most of the events.' She knew the events had been scheduled to avoid clashes, allowing the participants to compete across multiple sports, but it also enabled Freddie to get to as many events as possible.

'But he'll meet the competitors at the Games. Will he meet us too?'

'There are a couple of family functions that I know Prince Alfred will be at. There is a barbecue on the first day and there is also the closing ceremony. I know there will be thousands of people there, but I will do my best.' She was determined to follow through with her promise. She knew it should be relatively easy for her to organise but she didn't divulge why.

'Okay, who's for a game of darts?' Mark asked. 'I know Viktoria would like to chat to the girls about their experiences and I don't think I want to hear all they have to say.'

Viktoria was surprised about how forthcoming the women were in sharing their stories and she was stunned to hear what they had been through. Their stories were all different, but the one common theme was how the Games had changed things for them. The Games had given their men hope and a purpose and turned things around for them mentally. Even Mark's girlfriend, who was new on the scene, had noticed a change in his self-esteem since he had begun training for the Games.

'How long have you been together?' Viktoria asked.

'Six months. What about you and Cam? Your relationship must be new.'

'We are not dating.'

'Oh, I thought—'

'Cam hasn't dated anyone since Gemma,' Lisa said.

Viktoria's immediate thought was *Who is Gemma?* And she was about to ask when Mark's girlfriend said, 'Gemma? I don't remember a Gemma. Did I meet her?'

'No. They were dating when he was in Afghanistan.'

'But that was years ago.'

Viktoria saw the look Lisa exchanged with Eric's wife, but it was fleeting and she couldn't decipher it before it was lost. She wanted to ask more but they changed the subject, leaving Viktoria to wonder about the mysterious Gemma and what she meant to Cam. Leaving her wondering about what had happened between them. Did their breakup have something to do with the helicopter incident? Was it too much for Gemma to handle? Had she not wanted to wait for

Cam to recover or to nurse him back to health? Did Cam break up with her? Or did he have his heart broken? He must have if he hadn't dated for years.

Viktoria was lost in her thoughts. The conversation continued around her and she decided it was time for her to leave.

She stood up to say goodbye just as Cam returned to the table with another round of drinks.

'Thank you,' she said as he passed her a glass of wine, 'but I think I am going to say goodnight.'

'Already?'

She nodded. It was time to go. Everyone had been very welcoming, but her mind was spinning.

'Can I give you a lift?'

She hesitated only fractionally, wondering if he'd really like to stay, before deciding that he had made the offer and she wanted to accept. '*Merci*, I would like that.' It would give her a chance to spend more time with Cam and maybe even learn more about him.

'Is everything okay?' he asked her as he slid behind the wheel after helping her into his car.

Had he picked up on her sombre mood?

'I had not fully understood the impact on the families. It was a little overwhelming, if I am honest.'

She was also feeling conflicted about her own self-indulgence. She had been bemoaning the fact that she was bored of handing out trophies and attending charity functions while these men and women had suffered real hardships and still managed to smile. The only real adversity she had faced was when Luca cheated on her and she broke off their engagement. That had been a difficult period in her life, but a broken heart was not normally fatal. She had experienced nothing like the stories she'd heard tonight, and she was awed by the strength and resilience they had all shown.

'I'm not sure how they manage to stay so positive,' she added.

'They've been through a lot,' Cam agreed.

She wondered what Cam's experiences were. And she wondered about Gemma.

She was desperate to know more, for Cam to open up to her, but she knew that he might then expect her to reciprocate and she wasn't sure what she wanted to tell him. What did she want him to know about her? There was so much she wanted to keep secret and she knew that wasn't fair. She couldn't expect him to disclose his past if she wasn't prepared to do the same but she was enjoying the opportunity to be a regular person, the chance to find out who she was without a crown or a royal title, and that was enough to persuade her to continue to keep her own counsel.

Cam pulled into the hotel driveway behind a long line of taxis. There was an empty parking bay on their left and Viktoria got Cam to turn into it. 'I can get out here,' she said.

She wondered if she was brave enough to invite him to come in but then decided against it. Hearing about Gemma had confused her. What had happened between them? Was Cam in a position where he might want to explore things with her or was he still not over Gemma? His friends had said he hadn't dated for years. What reason did she have to think he would be ready now? He was hard to read, and she didn't want to make a fool of herself.

She would err on the side of caution.

'Thank you for the lift,' she said as she leant across and kissed him on his left cheek followed by the right.

Their faces were close, their cheeks still

touching, and in the dim interior of the car his eyes were dark and hard to read.

They moved simultaneously, together or apart she wasn't quite sure, but suddenly it wasn't her cheek under his lips any more but her mouth. His lips covered hers and she heard herself sigh as she closed her eyes. His lips were warm and soft, but his pressure was firm. She opened her mouth and tasted him.

She lost herself in the kiss. Oblivious to anything and everything else, completely unaware of their surroundings, forgetting who she was, where she was, as she kissed him back. She didn't care who saw her. She couldn't have stopped if she'd wanted to. The kiss was everything she had imagined.

Viktoria felt as if she was floating as she made her way into the hotel. She still wasn't sure who had kissed who, but she didn't care. It didn't matter. What mattered was that it had been a perfect kiss and that he had asked her to spend the morning with him tomorrow.

He might not want to date but that hadn't stopped him from asking her to meet him at

Bondi Beach at sunrise. It had been a perfect kiss and tomorrow had the potential to be the perfect day.

CHAPTER FOUR

SUNRISE WAS CAM'S favourite time of day at the beach. Seeing the sun come up over the ocean was the best start to a day and there were still many days when he really needed to see that. It served as a reminder to him that life went on.

Bondi wasn't his favourite beach. He found it too crowded and he normally avoided it but he was prepared to make an exception today. He was prepared to make an exception after the events of last night.

He had kissed Viktoria. Or she had kissed him. He wasn't sure how that had happened and at the time he hadn't thought too much of it. He'd just enjoyed the moment and then heard himself invite her to Bondi. It was almost as if she had cast a spell over him and he knew he had to see her again. Wanted to see her again.

But once he got home the doubts began.

Was he making a mistake?

Once again, it was too late. He seemed to be going about things in the wrong order with Viktoria. Speaking first and thinking later. Inviting her out and then wondering if he should have. Kissing her and then wondering if he should have. Maybe he needed to start counting to ten. He knew he was thinking with his heart instead of his head. Somehow, she was able to make him forget his guilt. Forget Gemma. And that was where the battle began. He didn't know if forgetting was the right thing to do.

Though he couldn't deny that he'd enjoyed the kiss. That for the first time in two years he'd been left wanting more.

But he was worried. At the moment she didn't know his history. He could pretend he was undamaged. But what if she got to know him and didn't like what she saw?

He hadn't intended to let his guard down and, while it was still up to a degree, he knew there were definite cracks in his walls. He'd taken her to his house. He'd cooked her dinner. And he'd invited her to spend the morning with him.

He liked the way he felt around her, but he didn't know if she would say the same. He wanted to be the best version of himself for her. Strong and intelligent. Not grumpy and damaged.

He wanted her to like him.

So, because he wanted Viktoria's approval, because he wanted to see her smile, he found himself at Bondi at sunrise. He knew Viktoria wanted to see the famous stretch of sand and he wanted to show it to her. He particularly wanted her to experience it at this time of day, when it was peaceful, before it was invaded by hordes of tourists and families. In his opinion that was a whole other experience, iconic maybe, but not nearly as pleasant.

The Bondi lifeguards were just setting up for duty, but the beach was virtually empty. The early risers were in the water, swimming, surfing, paddling and Cam caught a wave and let it carry him back into the shore. He shook his head, spraying water across the sand, and rubbed his hair with his towel to stop the water from dripping down his back, and headed for the lifeguard tower where he'd arranged to meet her. He didn't want her to be there before him.

She was walking towards him. She had her hair pulled up into a bun today, but he was only vaguely aware of that. She was dressed in shorts and a loose top. Her shorts were very short and her legs were amazing. She was coming out of a northern hemisphere summer and her legs were slim and tanned. Cam had to force himself to keep his eyes up.

'Bonjour.' She greeted him with a kiss on each cheek. Left then right. Just like last night but this time there was nothing extra and Cam forced himself to push the disappointment to the back of his mind. Today was about showing Viktoria one of the iconic Australian sights; it was about spending time with her, not about his desires. But he couldn't deny that she had stirred something in him. Reawakened his desires. It had been years since he had felt such strong attraction and he had to admit he was actually excited to see what might develop. Would she be the one who helped him move on?

Was he ready to let go of the past?

He was tired of thinking and he was tired of feeling guilty. He wanted to feel happy and maybe, just maybe, Viktoria could help him achieve that.

Her skin was warm and soft against his cheek and she smelt incredible. 'Good morning,' he replied. 'Welcome to Bondi.'

She grasped the railing that overlooked the beach with both hands and leant over, looking up and down the beach. 'I cannot believe I am here!' She turned back to face him, a wide smile on her face, and Cam's day got even better. 'I must take a photo.'

She pulled her phone from the pocket of her shorts and turned her back to the beach, holding her phone up, ready to take a selfie with the beach behind her.

'Why don't you let me take one of you?' he offered.

'No,' she said as she grabbed hold of his hand and pulled him closer. 'You have to be in it also.' She stepped in front of him slightly, tucking herself into the curve of his shoulder, and pressed back against him. Her bottom pressed against his hip, testing his self-control. She extended her arm and looked at the screen. 'Step to your right a little,' she instructed.

He did as she asked and saw that she now had the edge of the round tower in the corner of the frame with the beach and ocean behind them. He wasn't sure that the light was right—the sun was still rising over the sea—but Viktoria snapped a photo and then adjusted the settings until she was happy with the result.

'There.' She held her phone out to him, showing him the picture.

She looked stunning. He looked a mess. He was only half smiling and he knew that was because he was trying so hard not to think about her body pressing up against his.

'*D'accord.* Are we going to swim?'

She shoved her phone back into her pocket and lifted her arms above her head, removing her top in one smooth movement to reveal a black bikini top. It was small but not skimpy, and she was probably in no danger of losing it in the notorious Bondi surf, but it was still only barely covering her, and Cam fought hard to maintain the last bit of self-control.

He definitely needed to get into the water.

'Or have you already been in without me?' she asked as she stuffed her top into the small bag she carried. She was looking at him, taking in his damp hair, bare chest and wet shorts, and he felt himself growing warm under her scrutiny.

He nodded. 'I thought I'd get my exercise in first. The water is cool, and I didn't know how long you'd want to stay in for.'

'How cool?'

'About twenty degrees.'

'That is okay. I need to go in; I have to be able to say I went swimming at Bondi.'

She skipped down the steps and onto the

sand. 'It's beautiful. I thought the beaches at home were lovely, but this is huge and the sand is so soft! Our beaches have a lot of rocks and the sand is coarse. They are nothing like this.'

Cam dropped his towel on the sand near where the lifeguards were positioning the red and yellow flags to mark the safe swimming zone.

'Are we just going to leave our things here?' Viktoria asked.

He looked up and down the almost deserted beach. 'It's safe enough,' he said. 'Anyone on the beach at this time of the day is more interested in getting their exercise done than in stealing stuff.'

She stepped out of her shorts and piled her things with his and followed him into the sea. Cam dived under a small wave and swam away from the beach, keen to get back into the cold water. He turned and looked back at Viktoria. She was wading in slowly, gradually getting in deeper, until she finally gathered her courage and pushed off the sandy bottom and swam breaststroke out to him. She was treading water to stay afloat.

'Hold on to me,' Cam told her. He was still able to touch the bottom.

She wrapped her arms around his shoulders and floated off him. He was aware of each of her ten fingertips pressing into his skin. Tiny little circles of heat. They faced the beach and the morning sun reflected off the windows of the houses. They could hear the waves breaking on the shore but otherwise it was peaceful. They didn't talk but it was a comfortable silence.

The surfers were all at the southern end of the beach and only a few lone swimmers shared their patch of the ocean. Cam watched one man whose strokes looked a little laborious. He did not look like a natural swimmer. He wasn't making a lot of headway and when he lifted his head he barely cleared the surface. Cam saw him swallow a mouthful of water before stopping and coughing. He sunk under the waves and Cam waited for him to come back up.

He did. But only briefly before he disappeared a second time.

His hand broke the surface but only momentarily and Cam knew he was in strife.

'Viktoria…there's a swimmer in trouble.' He pointed towards the spot where he'd last seen the man, knowing even as he did there was nothing for Viktoria to see. He waved his arm, signalling to the lifeguards, but it was impossible to know if they had seen him. The man had swum out wider than the red and yellow flags; he was out of the manned zone. 'He needs help. I'm going to swim over to him. Can you get out of the water and run to the lifeguard tower? Can you do that?'

'*Oui*,' She didn't question him. She let go of him and kicked away, swimming free-style towards the beach as Cam sprinted in the opposite direction. He wasn't sure that he knew exactly where the man had been, but he would try his best to find him. Even if the lifeguards had seen him there was no certainty that they would be any more accurate.

Cam swam a dozen strokes and then dived under the water, searching for the man.

Nothing.

He swam a dozen more, faster this time, and dived again.

This time he saw him, suspended under the surface.

Cam cut through the water and grabbed the man under the armpits. He was unconscious, a heavy, dead weight even in the buoyant saltwater.

Cam hauled him to the surface and used one hand to cup the man's chin and hold his head out of the water as he kicked sideways and aimed for the beach. He was out of breath by the time he was waist deep. His feet hit the bottom and he dragged the man into the shallows, laying him on the wet sand.

He looked up. Viktoria was still running towards the lifeguards; she was on the soft sand, making hard work of the distance. She should have stuck to the firm sand, but she was too far away to hear him if he called out to her. The tower was a long way from the northern end of the beach and the smaller north tower wasn't manned unless the beach was busy, but he could see lifeguards responding now. They had seen Viktoria and were sprinting for the buggy.

Cam turned his attention back to the unconscious man. He guessed him to be in his early sixties. He was slightly overweight but not in bad shape. If you ignored the fact that he wasn't breathing.

Cam pressed his fingers to the man's neck. There was no pulse.

He rolled him onto his side to clear his airway before rolling him back onto his back so he could start CPR. The man was in cardiac arrest and time was critical. He started compressions, counting in his head as he kept one eye on the buggy and the lifeguards.

Thirteen, fourteen.

The buggy stopped to pick up Viktoria.

Seventeen, eighteen.

It was racing along the sand now.

Twenty-nine, thirty.

He stopped compressions and gave the man two breaths.

The buggy came to a halt and two lifeguards jumped out.

Cam kept the compressions going as he counted to thirty again.

'Are you okay to continue the compressions?' one of them asked as he knelt beside Cam. 'I'll do the breaths.'

Cam nodded. The other lifeguard was readying the defibrillator.

He sat back as he got to thirty, allowing the lifeguard to attach the leads while the second one breathed air into the man's lungs.

The defibrillator charged, preparing to shock.

'All clear. Shock now.'

They waited for the result.

Nothing.

Cam continued compressions as the defibrillator prepared itself again.

'I'll take over after the next shock, if needs be,' one of the lifeguards told Cam.

Cam nodded in acknowledgement as he kept counting.

The defibrillator shocked the man again. But again, there was no response.

Cam stood up, leaving the man in the care of the lifeguards. He could hear sirens in the distance and knew the ambulance was on its way.

A crowd had gathered. Joggers, dog walkers and swimmers surrounded them, and Cam wondered where they had all come from. The beach had seemed virtually deserted ten minutes ago. He could see Viktoria at the back of the crowd, her hand pressed to her mouth, her face pale.

He went to her as the lifeguards continued to work on the man.

She was shivering. He wrapped his arms around her, trying to calm her, to warm her, to reassure her. Her skin was cold, but he knew she was probably also in shock.

'*Mon Dieu!* Is he going to be all right?'

'I don't know,' Cam said. The man's prospects were not good, but it was clear that Viktoria was already overwhelmed and he knew there was nothing to be gained by giving her more bad news. What she was witnessing was already traumatic enough.

Viktoria leaned into Cam as he wrapped his arms around her. She was shaking and Cam rubbed her arms, trying to warm her up, but she wasn't sure that it was the cold making her tremble.

His skin was warm in contrast to hers; the physical exertion of performing resuscitation had warmed him. He felt solid and safe and comforting. She needed the comfort.

'Come on. You need to get warm.'

A large crowd had gathered and she was finding the situation confronting and she was relieved when Cam led her away. She had never witnessed anything like that before and wasn't in any hurry to prolong the experience.

'What about the man?' she asked as she let Cam lead her away from the crowd.

'There's nothing more we can do.'

'Are they going to be able to revive him?'

'I really don't know. It's not looking too good.'

He picked their towels up from the sand and wrapped one around her shoulders, but he continued to hold her close as they made their way to the lifeguard tower. He left his details there in case they needed to speak to him before he bundled her into his car and turned the heating up.

'Where are we going?' she asked as he pulled out of the parking space.

'I thought I'd take you to my place. It's closer than your hotel. You'll feel better after a hot shower and something to eat.'

She didn't think she could stomach any food, but a hot shower sounded divine.

She kept her eyes averted as they drove past the ambulance.

'Are you okay?' Cam asked her.

She nodded. 'I think so. I have never seen a dead person before. I do not think it is something I will forget.'

'No,' he agreed. 'Those images can be hard to get out of your head. But, in my experience, it's easier when you don't know the person.'

'I am sorry. Being in the army, you have probably seen much worse. You have lost friends?'

'I have.'

She reached across and put her hand on his thigh, offering him comfort this time. He turned his head and gave her a brief half-smile.

He seemed lost in his thoughts and she

wondered if they were solely to do with the drowning man or if there was more going through his head. Was he thinking about his friends? Who had he lost?

She would love to know more but she didn't want to pry. She knew how it felt to be the subject of gossip and speculation but that didn't stop her thinking about Gemma again.

What had happened to her? Where had she gone? Was she one of the people he'd lost? Why had she and Cam broken up?

Cam had kissed her but what if he'd been thinking about Gemma? What if he regretted the kiss? Had it reminded him of Gemma? Brought back memories? She wished, almost desperately, that she knew what he was thinking, what he was feeling, but it was impossible to tell and she could go crazy trying to figure it all out.

She knew he was making an effort for her. She would cope. She wouldn't dwell on the unknowns, about the man on the beach or Cam's exes. She'd be upbeat and lift the mood.

'So what are we going to do to cheer ourselves up?' she asked.

'I'll think of something,' he said as he

turned into his driveway, 'but first a shower and some dry clothes.'

Rex greeted them at the door, his tail wagging, and Viktoria immediately felt her spirits lift as she bent down and rubbed his head.

Cam showed her to the bathroom. He handed her fresh towels and said, 'You should have everything you need in there. Take your time; I'll make a start in the kitchen.'

She was tempted to drag him into the shower with her. She thought they could possibly both benefit from the distraction, but she wasn't sure what mood he was in. He was so difficult to read, sometimes looking as if he had the weight of the world on his shoulders. She realised he was probably feeling bad about the events of the morning, but they hadn't been his doing. He probably thought she was still in shock. She knew she'd be fine.

She washed and semi-dried her hair. She could smell coffee brewing and decided her hair could finish drying while she got her caffeine fix.

Cam had laid the table outside by the pool. 'I wasn't sure what you would like. There's coffee, smashed avocado on toast and poached eggs. Take a seat and help yourself.'

She didn't normally eat breakfast and forty minutes ago she would have thought she couldn't handle any food but it felt as if she'd been up for hours and the combination of a swim and the fresh air had left her ravenous, despite the unfortunate events.

A light breeze blew across the deck and, despite the sun, she could feel goose bumps on her skin; the air was fresh after the heat of the shower.

Cam disappeared into the house and when he returned he handed her a soft, well-worn top. 'Here, put this on, or we could eat inside if you prefer?'

'*Non, merci.* This will be perfect,' she said as she took the offered jumper. She slipped it over her head and rolled up the sleeves. It was soft and well-loved and she imagined it smelt of Cam. Wearing his top was like being wrapped in his arms again.

Cam spread some avocado on a slice of toasted bread, squeezed a little lemon juice on and added some cracked pepper. 'Try this,' he said as he passed it to her. 'It's an Aussie speciality.'

She pushed the sleeves of his jumper up her arm and took the toast. She looked adorable in his jumper and all he wanted to do was take her in his arms and remove it. No matter how good she looked in it, he knew he'd prefer to see her in nothing at all. He was unsettled. Pleasantly unsettled.

He was attracted to her and he wasn't at all sure what to do about it. He hadn't felt like this in a long time. There was something different about her. Being in her company felt different to the other dates he had been on but, as yet, he hadn't been able to figure out why.

Perhaps it was because she made him remember his old self. How he'd been before the accident. He felt lighter. Freer. Maybe even happy. And it was nice to have some company, other than Rex.

And the kiss had been phenomenal. And he wanted to do it again.

That was also new.

He was fighting a battle between guilt and desire and he didn't know which would win.

'This is delicious,' Viktoria said as she finished the smashed avocado and licked her fingers clean.

Cam tried to make conversation as he also tried to ignore the way her lips curled around her fingers. 'What are your plans for this afternoon?' he asked.

'I have none.'

'I'm going to visit my sister this afternoon; she lives on a property about ninety minutes away. Would you like to come with me? It would give you a chance to see something other than the city.'

He told himself he was asking because he was worried about her being alone after the morning's events. He felt responsible for her, given the shock she'd had this morning. But he also knew he wanted her to keep him company.

'Are you sure?'

'She has horses,' he said, hoping that would convince her. She had told him she loved to ride.

'Well, then, of course I would love to come. Is this the sister who gave you Rex?'

'It is. I only have one sister.'

'And she lives so far away?'

'It's only a little more than one hundred kilometres away. That's not far in Australia.'

'If I was at home a one-hundred-kilometre drive would put me in another country!' she exclaimed. 'Either France or Spain. Berggrun is only six thousand square kilometres in size. Half the size of Sydney. Two hours' drive is about as far as you can go before you find yourself out of the country.'

'We might not get into another state, but it will feel a world away.'

The city had given way to green fields, grapevines and small country towns and Viktoria was as excited as a young child at Christmas to see kangaroos with joeys in the bush as they drove past. Eventually Cam turned off the highway and drove over a cattle grid between white wooden fence posts. Horses grazed in the paddocks on either side of the driveway, but they were a breed Viktoria didn't recognise.

'What sort of horses are they?' she asked.

'Walers,' Cam replied. 'My sister and her husband breed them.'

He drove past the stables and up to the house. It was built of stone but clearly modern, with large windows that looked over the paddocks. A steel pergola, covered in vines, jutted out from the front of the house.

A heavily pregnant woman with dark hair stepped out of the house as Cam pulled his SUV to a stop.

Cam opened Viktoria's door for her before greeting the woman with a hug.

'Hello, little brother,' she said as she let go of Cam and smiled at Viktoria.

Cam introduced them. 'This is my sister,

Skye, and her husband, David.' Skye had the same blue-grey eyes as Cam. David was a tall, solidly built man with sandy hair and a pleasant face.

'Hello, Viktoria,' Skye welcomed her. 'I hear you've had rather an eventful day.'

Viktoria handed Skye the bouquet of flowers that she had bought from a roadside stall during the drive. She'd insisted that Cam stop, knowing she couldn't arrive both uninvited and empty-handed. '*Oui*, a little more stressful than I am used to, *certainement*. Thank you for including me this afternoon; I know you were not expecting me.'

'Don't be silly. Friends of Campbell's are always welcome.'

Viktoria didn't miss the sideways glance Skye gave Cam and she wondered what it was all about.

She followed Skye into the house, stepping straight into a large living room adjacent a modern kitchen.

'And I agree with Cam,' Skye said as she filled a vase with water and arranged the flowers. 'You had a nasty shock this morning; it is better not to be on your own. Although he could have postponed the visit instead of dragging you out into the countryside.'

'I was happy to come. I must admit, I might have invited myself. I wanted to see something of the country and, once Cam told me you had horses, I was not going to let him cancel his visit.'

'Do you ride?'

'*Oui.*' She had ridden almost before she could walk.

'Would you like to see the horses?'

'I would love to.'

'Perfect. I'll leave the men to sort afternoon tea and I'll take you to see the animals. The two of you can handle that, can't you?' she asked, looking from David to Cam and back again. 'Boil the kettle and cut some cake; we won't be long.'

Skye peppered Viktoria with questions as they wandered down to the paddocks. 'You're working at the Games? Is that where you met Cam?'

'*Oui.* He had to show me around the event venues. He was not too happy about that, but I hope he has forgiven me the inconvenience.'

'I imagine he has.' Skye turned her head and gave her another look that she wasn't able to decipher. 'Are you living in Australia or just here for the Games?'

'Just for the Games. I only have ten more days.'

'Ah, I see.'

Viktoria wondered what that meant. She was having trouble deciphering Skye's language. She had thought Cam was hard to read but it seemed his sister was just as difficult. Perhaps it ran in the family.

Skye reached into a plastic tub and pulled out several apples. Immediately the horses came to the fence.

'Cam said they are called Walers,' Viktoria said as she fed the apples to the horses. 'I have never heard of them. They don't look like thoroughbreds.'

'No, they're not. They are heavier. Stronger. They're an Australian horse,' Skye explained, 'A mix of thoroughbred, Arab, the Cape horse from Africa, the Timor pony and, most likely, a little bit of Clydesdale as well, but they originated here in New South Wales—hence the name. Have you ever heard of the Australian Lighthorsemen?'

'From the War, *oui*?'

'Yes. They used Walers. They were bred as stock horses initially but then used for the military because they were so tough and strong. There are some amazing stories of their efforts in both the Boer War and the First World War.'

'You have so many. What do you do with them?'

'We sell them. Mainly as stock horses but we've sold a few recently to be used as therapy animals.'

'I have heard of therapy dogs,' Viktoria said, recalling Fiona and her dog, Leroy, 'but I have not heard of therapy horses.'

'Some horses develop a good relationship with people if they have the right temperament. Walers form strong attachments. I breed them and then they go to stables around the country and people suffering from depression and PTSD and the like can spend time with them. Some ride, some just like to brush them, to talk to them. The horses don't judge.'

Viktoria was fascinated. 'And who looks after the horses? Do you need special training?'

'No. You just need to know how to look after a horse and once you get to know the horse's personality, and they know yours, you'll have a friend for life.'

'And this is something you have always done?'

'Not exactly. Cam and I grew up on a

sheep station. Naturally, we learnt to ride, and I bred some horses when I was younger but nothing serious. Neither Cam nor I wanted to inherit the sheep station so when our parents sold it to retire and move into town, I spent my inheritance on this property and Cam bought his house.'

'Does he ride?' Viktoria asked. Cam hadn't mentioned riding when they'd spoken of the horses. She'd told him she rode but she hadn't gone into detail. It was another one of the things she had kept quiet.

'Not any more,' Skye said as she handed over the last apple and put the lid on the tub. She wiped her hands on her apron and said, 'We should get back for afternoon tea before the boys eat all the cake.'

Once again Viktoria had the feeling of things unspoken.

They had spent a pleasant afternoon with Skye and David, but Viktoria had been keen to be alone with Cam again. Freddie was due to arrive in Sydney tomorrow and she suspected that might curtail her freedom. She wouldn't be able to disappear on a whim. She had messaged Brigitta to let her know she was spending the afternoon with Cam but while Brigitta could track her movements through an app on her phone she wouldn't question Viktoria's decisions. Freddie might be more interested in the company she was keeping.

As Cam turned into the hotel driveway she decided she would ask if he wanted their day to continue. He would either say yes or no.

'Are you going to walk me up to my room?' she asked as the doorman approached.

She waited. There was no pretending that either of them didn't know what she was asking, and she wasn't getting out of the car until she had his answer.

He switched off the engine, stepped out of the car and handed the keys to the valet attendant.

She smiled and took his hand and led him to the private lift that would take them directly to her penthouse. If he noticed that she had her own lift, he didn't comment. They stepped out into the foyer of the penthouse and she swiped her access key again to let them into the living room. The curtains were open, and Sydney Harbour glittered in the twilight.

'Is this what working for a prince looks like?' he asked as he took in his surroundings. He wandered over to the floor-to-ceiling windows. 'Please tell me the charitable trust isn't paying for this.'

He had his back to her as he looked out to the water and she quickly messaged Brigitta to tell her that she was back but didn't want to be interrupted and she would let her know if she needed her before she replied to Cam. 'It is not. But I did not invite you up here to look at *that* view.'

As she hoped, that got his attention.

He turned to find that she had kicked off her shoes and had her fingers on the top button of her shirt.

He crossed the room in three strides as she undid the first button.

His grey eyes were dark, and his gaze was unwavering. She could see her own desire reflected in his eyes and she felt her temperature rise as a flush stole over her cheeks and anticipation burned bright inside her. She couldn't breathe; his gaze was so intense it felt as if the room lacked oxygen, as if it was being burnt up in his eyes. She parted her lips to take a breath.

Her lips felt dry, her throat parched. She licked her lips with the tip of her tongue as Cam groaned and gave in to his desire. Gave in to hers.

He wrapped one arm around her back and

pulled her to him and kissed her hard. He tasted of coffee and cinnamon, of freedom and promises.

She reached one hand behind his head, holding him to her as she kissed him back. His tongue was warm in her mouth. His hands were warm on her skin. Every inch of her was on fire, consumed with desire. She felt his fingers on her arm, could feel them tracing a line up to her shoulder, across her collarbone to the sweet hollow at the base of her throat. She felt his thumb dip into the little dimple. She couldn't breathe; she'd forgotten how.

She needed to breathe.

She pulled away and he lifted his hand, releasing her from his touch. She almost begged him not to. She didn't want him to let her go.

'Are you okay?' he asked.

She nodded, unable to speak but, aware that the curtains were still open, she knew they needed to move into the privacy of her bedroom. She knew it was unlikely, but she couldn't ignore the fact that paparazzi were everywhere and, even though no one seemed to have worked out who she was, old habits died hard. She knew all about photographers with long camera lenses and she couldn't afford to take the chance.

She took his hand and led him into the bedroom. She hit the button on the remote to draw the sheer curtains across the windows, giving them some privacy without total darkness.

She wound her arms around his neck and pulled him close. His gaze ran over her face before moving lower, over her breasts. How could grey eyes hold such heat? Such intensity? She held her breath, trying to stop the rise and fall of her breasts, but still her nipples peaked in response to his gaze burning through the thin fabric of her shirt. She could feel the moisture between her legs as her body responded as his gaze devoured her. He'd scarcely laid a finger on her and yet she felt ready to self-combust. A look, a glance, a smile was all it would take for her to melt under him.

'Are you sure about this?'

Again, there was no pretending they didn't know exactly what he was asking.

'Yes.' Her voice was breathless. She wasn't going to pretend that they hadn't been leading up to this moment all day. 'I want you to make love to me.'

She didn't need to ask twice.

His fingers found the buttons on her shirt and he undid them in seconds. He bent his head and trailed a line of kisses from her collarbone to the swell of her breast. Her legs trembled, threatening to give way, but before she could stumble he scooped her up with one arm and lifted her onto the bed.

She lay back as he eased himself over her, supporting himself on his elbows. She reached up and ran her hands over his biceps, feeling his strength, marvelling at the firmness within him. His breath was coming fast now, she could hear it and feel it as it hit the bare skin of her shoulders and neck, but he didn't move. How could he hold himself so still? He was poised to move forward, to take this to the next level, but somehow he held his position. He was in no hurry. How could he be so calm when desire threatened to consume her?

The waiting was exquisite agony. A delicious sense of anticipation battled with the desire to have him take her now, right now. She arched her hips up towards him, pushing herself against his groin, and was rewarded when she felt his matching desire, hard and firm, straining against his pants.

She breathed out on a sigh as she let her knees fall open and wrapped her legs around him, pulling him closer, pulling him down against her. She heard him groan and he lowered his body until it covered the length of her. She wanted this. She wanted to feel his weight on her; she needed to know this was real.

Every cell of her body tingled in anticipation; she could feel each one straining, reaching out to him. Her skin was on fire and every nerve ending quivered with anticipation, alive with the possibilities of what was to come. Her expectations were almost painful, her reaction intense.

He reached for her, ending her suspense. His lips were on her earlobe, soft and warm, his breath in her ear. He kissed her neck and then his lips covered hers and she melted into him and let him consume her.

His fingers skimmed over her nipples, hard and peaked. He swept the strap of her bra from her shoulder and exposed her left breast to the cool air. His thumb brushed over her nipple, teasing, tantalising. She cried out as a wave of desire washed over her and a bolt of heat scorched through her, sweeping from her nipple to her groin in a searing flash.

His hands slid behind her back and with an expert flick of his fingers he undid her bra. He bent his head and his lips left a trail of hot spots from her lips to her throat and collarbone until finally he took the tip of her breast in his mouth, rolling his tongue over the taut flesh until Viktoria thought she might come then and there. But she didn't want it to end. Not yet. Maybe not ever. She wanted to feel him, to touch him, to arouse him too.

Her hands found the bottom of his T-shirt and she pushed it up until she could run her hand over his warm skin. His skin was firm but soft under her fingertips. She pulled his shirt from his body as his mouth continued to tease her nipple, sucking and licking. He paused momentarily to let her drag his shirt over his head before he returned his attention to her and her pleasure.

He cupped her breast in his hand and ran his thumb over the peaked bud, making her moan. She arched her back, offering herself to him, and he took one peak in his mouth again, sucking hard, and she almost exploded in his arms.

She ran her index finger from his sternum down along the line separating his abdominal muscles, following the line of dark hair that led below his waistband. She concentrated on him, wanting to extend the pleasure, wanting to share the delight. She snapped open the button on his trousers, unzipping his fly and pushing his pants low on his hips. His erection strained against the fabric of his boxer shorts. She ran her hand over his shaft; it was strong and thick, and she felt it rise to meet her. He groaned and the sound of his arousal urged her on.

His hand ran up her thigh and under the hem of her shorts. She pushed against him and instructed, 'Take them off.'

She lifted her hips as he undid her shorts and slid them off. His fingers met the elastic of her underwear and slid under the lace of her undies. Viktoria let her legs fall apart again, opening herself to him, giving herself to him, and she bit back a cry of desire as his fingers slid inside her. She was slick and wet, throbbing. His thumb found her centre and she gasped as his touch took her to the edge.

But she didn't want it this way. She wanted to share the experience. She wanted all of him and she wanted him to have all of her. She let go of him and pulled her underwear off and lay naked before him. His blue-grey eyes roamed over her body, setting her on fire with his gaze.

She watched as he stood and divested

himself of his pants and shoes. She didn't think she could bear to wait much longer. She was desperate to feel him inside her. Desperate for them to be joined together.

To know that he wanted her as much as she wanted him.

Cam looked at Viktoria lying on the bed, naked, waiting, and he pushed aside any reservations. He hadn't made love to anyone since Gemma, but it was too late for any doubts. He didn't want to think; he couldn't think. There was no room in his head for anything other than desire. It took all his self-control to hold back long enough to find his wallet and retrieve a condom.

She lay, propped on her elbows, naked and gorgeous, and watched him roll it on.

She reached for his hand and pulled him back onto the bed. She reached behind him, holding his hips, cupping his buttocks, to pull him close. She arched her back and let her knees fall open as she fitted him to her like pieces of a jigsaw.

She sighed as he thrust into her.

She gave herself to him and he claimed her. All of her.

He filled her, consumed her and they became one.

Cam felt himself losing control.

Everything else in his life was forgotten as Viktoria took over his senses. He wanted to go slowly, he wanted to savour the moment, he wanted time to commit it all to memory, but he couldn't resist her. He couldn't fight it. He was only a man, a powerless man, and he could feel himself being swept away. The world ceased to exist except for Viktoria.

This was what he wanted. To disappear into a world of pleasure. To escape from a world of pain.

But Viktoria came into this new world with him. He wanted, needed to escape but he also wanted her to share in this moment with him. He was choosing to let her in.

And suddenly there was nothing else that mattered.

He wasn't thinking about the incident, or his scars, or his guilt or even Gemma. For the first time in years there was no room in his head for any of those things. He was completely in the present, immersed in the moment. The only thing he was thinking about was Viktoria.

He felt her hand on his chest, felt it brush over one nipple, felt another surge of blood to his groin. He breathed her name and that was the last coherent thought he had. Her legs wrapped around his waist, pinning him to her. She pushed her hips against his and his resistance crumbled.

She tilted her hips and moved in time with him. He heard his own guttural moan as he thrust into her, filling her, claiming her for his own. He couldn't hold back, he couldn't resist and when he heard her call his name it pushed him further.

There was nothing gentle in their lovemaking. It was fuelled by pure desire. Desperate, all-consuming desire.

He thrust into her again, up and down he moved, faster and faster, harder and stronger, and she met each thrust. She arched her back and held him close with her legs, opening herself to him, offering herself to him.

He buried himself deep inside her and when he felt her shudder and come undone, he came with her. They climaxed together and when they were completely spent he gathered her to him, holding her close, reluctant to let her go as he savoured this next moment, as they lay in each other's arms, slick with sweat and breathing hard.

She had blown his mind.

She had given him a gift. She had relieved him of his trauma and stress. He felt as if she had pieced a bit of him back together.

That while she held him in her embrace he was restored, renewed, revived.

For those minutes she had let him feel like the man he used to be and he wondered: Did she have the power, the ability to heal him, to restore him?

She lay curled against his side. Her fingers were warm as they trailed over his chest, across a nipple, down his sternum and over his abdomen, coming to rest on the scar on his hip bone.

He could feel himself stirring again as her hand moved lower. Following the line of his scar.

Down the outside of his thigh.

'How did you get this scar?'

Her question brought him abruptly back to reality.

He'd been kidding himself that he could stay in the bubble she'd created. He'd thought tonight might have been different. That it could be the turning point for him. But once again he was too quickly thrust back into his reality.

But this time there was a difference. This time he had been prepared to let someone in. And if he was going to let her in then she deserved an answer.

'I was involved in an incident.'

'It is a big scar. Was it a bad incident?'

'It was.' It couldn't have been worse. Even if he'd died too, he had thought at times that that would have been a better outcome. Guilt continued to eat at him. If everyone had died, including him, he wouldn't be living with that guilt. But he didn't say that.

'Was it a long time ago?'

'Two years.'

'Will you tell me about it?'

If she'd asked him if he wanted to talk about it he would have said no, but what did it matter if he told her about the incident? If she wanted to, she could find out all the information on the internet anyway. The articles didn't talk about the personal cost of the incident. The articles didn't mention how it had destroyed his life, and he didn't need to talk about that either, but he could give her the facts. He'd repeated them often enough in various hearings and in front of various panels.

But only a handful of people heard about his guilt—the psychologists, Doug, Skye.

But he wasn't ready to leave her yet. Talking to her was a way to stay beside her for a little longer.

'I was deployed to the Middle East as a surgeon,' he said. Lying in the semi-darkness made it easier to tell his story. 'I was responsible for medical treatments and surgery at the base hospital, but I also went out into the field with the helicopter evacuation unit to retrieve injured or wounded soldiers. I was almost due to come home when a retrieval went wrong.

'The helicopter crashed. It was shot down. I thought it must have been a mistake, but I found out later it was deliberate. They ignored the medical markings and launched missiles at us. I ended up with multiple injuries, including a fractured pelvis and a shattered femur. I was put back together with plates and pins and screws, which is where that scar came from. I lost a lot of blood, but people said I was lucky.'

'That does not sound lucky. That sounds painful.'

'They meant lucky to be alive.'

'Oh.'

He hadn't felt lucky. 'The chopper crashed and then caught fire. There were six people on board. I was the only survivor.'

'Everyone else died?'

He nodded. 'I couldn't get them out.' He still felt guilty. 'I couldn't stand, I couldn't breathe. I dragged myself out of the chopper, but I couldn't save anyone else.'

He'd been told later that the others had all died on or before impact, but he didn't know if he believed that. He still wondered if the army was telling him that to make him feel better.

He'd lain in the dirt for an hour before he'd been found.

Somehow, he'd survived. But for a long time he'd wished he'd died.

'Were they your friends?'

She had her head resting on his chest as her fingers made tiny circles over his abdominal muscles. Her breath was warm on his skin. Her deep, husky voice relaxed him, hypnotised him.

'They were more than that.'

He was aware of dampness on his cheeks. Tears. Tears for his colleagues. Tears for Gemma. He wiped them away with the back of his hand. He did not want to be sad, not tonight, and he didn't want Viktoria's pity.

He lifted her hand and kissed her fingers. He was done talking.

He wanted to forget the past. He wanted to stay in this moment in time. He was content, sated, and he wanted the feeling to last a little longer.

CHAPTER FIVE

THERE WAS NOT an empty seat in the basketball arena. Special platforms had been built to accommodate spectators in wheelchairs and every available seat and spot was taken. Wheelchair basketball was the first sport on the programme and expectations were high and nerves were taut——both for the competitors and the organising committee.

But first there was the opening welcome address from the Prince. His arrival was greeted by rousing applause, but Cam scarcely noticed. Viktoria arrived in the arena with the Prince and Cam only had eyes for her.

He hadn't seen her since he'd left her bed in the early hours of yesterday morning.

He had spent yesterday in meetings, discussing the final preparations for the games which began today. The irony of his situation wasn't lost on him. He had finally met someone he actually wanted to spend time with, and he was too busy. For once he hadn't wanted to throw himself into work. For once he had something else he'd rather be doing.

He had expected to feel some regret, but he didn't. He felt unburdened.

He'd thought he might have some reservations that he had revealed too much. But he didn't. He knew he hadn't revealed all. Fewer than a handful of people knew the whole truth.

He was standing courtside with the medical team and Viktoria came to stand by his side. He smiled at her. 'Good morning. Are you ready for this?'

'I think so. Are you?'

He nodded. He had done everything he could to prepare and now he had to hope he had covered all contingencies.

They stood in silence and listened as Doug introduced Prince Alfred.

The Prince strode to the microphone that had been assembled in the centre of the basketball court. He was tall, blond and physically fit but he had spoken previously about the effect that being part of combat missions had on him mentally and the crowd greeted and accepted him as one of their own. He was casually dressed, wearing a dark navy

Legion's Games polo shirt and pressed chinos. It was the same shirt that the English competitors wore and it gave the impression that, although he was royalty, he wasn't there as the Prince but simply as one of them. A returned soldier.

Viktoria held up her phone, preparing to video the Prince's opening address. There was a large media contingent courtside as well. Cam knew the Games would get a large amount of coverage, which could only be a good thing. Hopefully, the publicity would inspire others, both soldiers and civilians, to get involved in sport. Cam knew that was the Prince's aim.

'Thank you for that warm welcome,' Prince Alfred said as the applause that greeted him eased. 'I am thrilled to be in Australia for the third Legion's Games. My vision was to encourage wounded and ill soldiers from all collegiate nations to experience the healing power of sport. I know many of you strive for perfection and love a challenge and I believed the Games would provide a platform to inspire, encourage and challenge soldiers to participate in sport. I have seen for myself how fiercely competitive most defence force personnel are, but the Legion's Games are not just about the

competition; they are also about achieve-
ment, belonging and family. For many, if
not most of us, our units became our family and I know what it feels like to lose that
family through injury, illness or retirement
and how difficult that can be when it was
not by choice.

'The ideal of these Games is to bring people together. Perhaps these Games will re-
unite you with your defence force family or
perhaps they will give you an opportunity
to introduce your civilian family to your defence force family. I hope these Games give
you a chance to support and embrace one
another and feel part of something unifying.

'The Games are about more than medals.
Whether you are a competitor or a spectator, you have all achieved something just by
being here. Each and every one of you are
part of these Games.

'The success of the first two Legion's
Games surpassed my expectations and it
is fantastic to see the Games grow in size
and in recognition. This year there are one
thousand competitors from twenty nations
competing across a dozen different sports.
I know these Games will be a great success
because if there's one thing Australians do
exceptionally well it is host sporting events.

'I want to wish you all good health, good luck and good times with friends old and new.

Let the Games begin.'

His speech was greeted with thunderous applause and cheers from the crowd and Cam had to bend his head close to Viktoria's ear to make sure she could hear him. 'All right. I'm on deck now,' Cam said as the basketball teams from Australia and England took to the court. 'I'll catch up with you later?'

He wanted to stay with her but he needed to work.

He wanted to hold her, to take her hand and take her away to where it could be just the two of them. To somewhere he didn't have to worry about what to do next, to somewhere no one would expect anything of him, to somewhere with no responsibilities and no commitment. With nothing but the two of them.

He was under her spell and he had no idea how it had happened. How he'd gone so quickly from being irritated at the thought of having to chaperone her to completely enamoured.

It wasn't like him to fall so fast. He was measured. Controlled. Sensible.

They'd shared one night and two days. It was crazy but he felt transformed.

Perhaps it was a good thing that he had to work. Perhaps he needed some time for his hormones to settle. For his emotions to calm down. His heightened emotions were usually of the fight kind—tense, wound tight. He wasn't used to this feeling of peace and calm. Of happiness. It was a little disconcerting.

Viktoria took her seat beside Freddie and quickly checked and uploaded the video of his welcome speech to the various digital platforms before settling in to watch the game.

The first game of the day was Australia v England, followed by USA v Canada. The stakes were high and the competition physical. The crowd got right behind the players and the stadium was filled with family and friends along with the team members of the other competing countries.

Flags from the twenty nations were hung throughout the stadium and the crowd was vocal, none more so than the Aussies with their popular, if uninventive, chant of, *'Aussie, Aussie, Aussie, Oi, Oi, Oi!'*

But Viktoria could see the attraction of

it—everyone knew the words! Even the other nations were getting into the spirit of the chant. But there was equal applause for the English team whenever they shot a basket or made a good play. The spirit of the Games was off to a great start.

Viktoria had never seen wheelchair basketball before, and she was surprised by how rough it was and how often the competitors were tipped out of their chairs.

Among all the action, she was also aware of Cam. She could see him across the court in the medical tent. Even though the base medical centre was only metres away in another building, first aid facilities had been established in each venue as well. Doctors were there to treat injuries, physios were busy taping and masseurs were on hand to relieve tired, cramping muscles.

Cam was busy but occasionally he glanced up at her and smiled. She couldn't help but smile back. She had come to Sydney for an adventure, but she was getting more than she had bargained for. She hadn't counted on meeting someone like Cam, but she intended to enjoy every minute of the experience. She would soon have to return to reality, to her real life.

The crowd gasped collectively, bringing her attention back to the court in front of her. One of the Aussie competitors had fallen hard. Viktoria recognised him as one of Mark's friends, one of the swim relay team, Bud.

She held her breath as his wheelchair was righted and he was escorted from the court. She could see him undergoing a concussion test in the medical tent and he didn't re-join the game, although he was able to go back onto the court at the end of the match when Freddie went to shake hands with all the players.

Cam came to sit next to her in the break.

'Is Bud okay?' she asked.

'He has a concussion. He might miss the next basketball game.'

'What about the swimming? The relay team sounds like it might be getting quite depleted.'

'As long as he can tell the deep end of the pool from the shallow end, he'll be okay.' Cam grinned at her. 'Have you got plans for tonight? I thought I could take you out for dinner.'

'I am having dinner with Fr—Prince Alfred.' She'd almost made a mistake. 'I am going to discuss my ideas with him.'

'Tomorrow night then?'

'*Oui*, I would like that.'

* * *

Viktoria was dining with Freddie when her mobile phone pinged with a message. She glanced at it and, when she saw it was Cam, picked it up to read it.

Let me know if he's boring you and you want to be rescued.

She smiled and texted back a quick reply.

'Who was that?'

'No one.'

'Come on, Viktoria. I know you better than that. Spill.'

Viktoria knew he would persist until she gave in and because she was more than happy to talk about Cam she filled Freddie in on the basics of the past few days.

'So, quite the adventure you're having,' her cousin said when she finished imparting the details she was happy to share. 'Are you going to tell him who you are?'

'No. That is not necessary. I will be gone in ten days. He does not need to know I am a princess. It does not matter.'

'Keeping secrets is never a good idea. I think you should tell him.'

'When I leave here I will be going home to get engaged. I will be getting married. I will not see him again so there is no need for him to know. I just want to be Viktoria for a few more days. That is all.'

'If you're sure.'

She had thought about telling Cam who she was, but she wasn't sure how he would take it. She didn't want it to change things between them. They didn't have a future together. It didn't matter that she had been picturing all sorts of alternative endings to her adventure in Australia, to what waited for her when she returned to Berggrun. Knowing that Cam was just the sort of man she could fall in love with—kind, considerate, intelligent and handsome—didn't mean anything.

He was also still guarded. She often had no idea about how he felt. She had no idea of his past. Of his plans for the future. Did he have any that could include her? She couldn't imagine him leaving everything he had here to follow her to Berggrun.

She needed to remember to treat this relationship as it was—a holiday romance—and not let herself get carried away with her dreams. She'd done that before with Luca and it had been a disaster.

The reality was that she was a reverse

Cinderella. She was a princess pretending to be ordinary and at the stroke of midnight, or in her case when she stepped onto the plane that would take her home, she would become royalty again.

She was worried that if she told him the truth, instead of Cinderella running from the ball it would be Cam.

She and Cam were from two different worlds. In her limited experience that did not get them off to a good start, no matter how intense their chemistry was. She could not imagine him anywhere but here.

His career was here. His family was here. Why would he leave all that behind for her? They barely knew each other. And it wasn't as if she could quit being a princess. No matter how much she might dream of doing exactly that, she knew it wasn't a realistic dream. It was a fantasy.

'Please don't say anything, Freddie.'

'Of course I won't. It's not my place. But I still think you should tell him.'

Dinner was at a restaurant overlooking Watson's Bay, a short walk from Cam's house. It was yet another perfect vista. Every corner she turned in Sydney seemed to bring her to another view of the water, another bay, another stretch of golden sand, more boats. Berggrun was a beautiful country, wealthy and with beautiful marinas, but it didn't have Sydney's stunning abundant natural beauty.

'Is every corner of Sydney as beautiful as the next?' she asked as the waiter took their orders.

'I haven't seen anything to compare to this view,' Cam told her, looking directly at her, his grey gaze so intense that she could feel herself blushing. 'I'm finding it hard to believe you are single.'

'I am definitely single.' For another few months at least. Until she turned thirty. 'I have been for several months. Since my ex-fiancé cheated on me.'

'You're kidding?'

'I wish I was. Or, at least, at the time I wished it was all a misunderstanding. Now I think I had a lucky escape.'

At the time she had believed Luca was the one for her but now she wondered if that was only because she was approaching her thirtieth birthday. There had always been red flags—he was charming and ambitious and selfish—but she had thought he'd loved her. She'd thought she'd loved him. But perhaps she'd been ignoring the warning signs, looking through rose-coloured glasses because in her head she knew she was expected to marry by the time she was thirty.

She wasn't sure if she'd really been in love with Luca or just in love with the idea of a fairy tale wedding.

But she'd learnt one thing from that experience—being a princess didn't guarantee a fairy tale ending.

'My brothers and Luca never got along. That should have been a warning sign for me. Next time I'll pay more attention.'

'You have brothers?'

'Two older brothers.'

For a moment she considered telling Cam who she really was, before deciding he didn't need to know. They wouldn't have a future and she didn't want to change anything between them at the moment. They only had a few more days together. 'So a holiday romance is just what I need to forget all about my disastrous love life.'

'And at the end of your holiday?'

'I have to go home. I have to be back in Berggrun for a family celebration. I leave the day after the Games.'

'So we will have to make the most of every minute,' Cam said as he signalled for the bill.

* * *

'Damn,' Cam said when they arrived home and he saw a car parked in his driveway.

'Whose car is that?'

'Skye's. I'd forgotten she was coming to stay.'

He didn't want to share this time with his sister. He didn't want family intruding. That was selfish but his thoughts were far from family. He only had one thing on his mind.

'You forgot?'

'I've been a bit preoccupied,' he said as he bent his head and kissed her. 'She hasn't come to see me; she has a doctor's appointment tomorrow. I think it must be her thirty-six-week check-up.'

'Should I get the hotel to send a car for me?'

'No.' It was late, and he hoped that Skye would have gone to bed already. Even before she'd got pregnant, she was an early to bed, early to rise person, always up at the crack of dawn with her horses. He was prepared to bet that she wouldn't be getting in their way.

He opened the door. The house was dark; just a single lamp was lit in the entry but there was a note on the kitchen bench from Skye.

Cam picked it up and breathed a sigh of relief. 'She's gone to bed.'

Viktoria stood behind him as he read the note. She pressed herself to his back and he felt her arms snake around his waist as she slid one hand under his shirt, her palm warm against his skin. He spun her around and pressed her back against the kitchen counter. He lifted her onto the benchtop. His hands cupped her buttocks. He pulled her towards him, and she wrapped her legs around his waist.

'What if Skye gets up?' she said before he could kiss her. 'I don't want her to see us here.'

Cam scooped her off the kitchen counter, lifting her easily, but she protested, 'Wait. Put me down. I can walk.'

'I've got you.' He wasn't about to let her go.

'But what about your leg? Let me walk.'

'My leg is fine.' He hadn't even thought about his leg and he certainly didn't want to be reminded of it. His door was ajar, and he kicked it open and carried her into his room.

He pushed the door closed with his foot and leant against it, letting Viktoria slide down until her feet touched the floor, but he kept his arms around her, keeping her pressed against him.

His breath was coming fast but it wasn't from exertion.

Her breaths were short and shallow too, her pupils large, as he bent his head and kissed her again.

CHAPTER SIX

VIKTORIA RAN HER hands under his shirt. She
trailed her fingernails lightly over his skin
and heard him moan. The room was in darkness but the curtains were open, letting the
moonlight spill in. His room faced the ocean
and, for once, Viktoria didn't worry about
the paparazzi. Cam's house was secluded
and private. She grabbed the bottom of his
shirt and pulled it over his head, exposing
his flat, toned stomach.

He started to undo his belt but Viktoria
stopped him.

'Let me,' she said. She undid his belt and
snapped open the button on his trousers before sliding the zip down. She could feel the
hard bulge of his erection pressing into her,
straining to get free.

Cam stepped out of his shoes, not both-
ering to untie the laces, as she pushed his
trousers to the floor. They joined his shoes

and shirt in an untidy heap. He was naked except for his underwear. Viktoria looked him over.

He was glorious.

He grinned at her and raised one eyebrow.

In silent reply, she put one hand on his smooth, broad chest and pushed him backwards until the bed bumped the back of his knees and made him sit. It was his turn to wait for her now.

She stepped back from the bed. Out of his reach. He could watch but he couldn't touch. She wanted to tease him. She reached for the zip at the side of her dress and undid it slowly. She slipped one strap from her shoulder and then the other and let the dress fall to the floor. Cam's eyes were dark grey now, as he watched and waited for her.

She reached her hands behind her back and unhooked her bra, sliding it along her arms and dropping it to the floor. She lifted her hands to her hair, to the elastic band that fastened the end of her plait and started to pull it from her hair.

'Wait. Let me do that.' Cam's voice was husky with desire. Lust coated his words, making them so heavy they barely made it past his lips.

Viktoria dropped her hand, leaving her hair restrained.

Cam reached up and his fingers rested at the nape of her neck before he flicked her plait over her left shoulder and pulled the elastic from her hair. He wound his fingers through her hair; loosening the plait, he spread her hair out, letting it fall over her shoulders.

His touch was light as he slid her underwear from her hips. Viktoria trembled with desire as his fingers skimmed her thighs. She stood before him, completely naked, but she didn't feel exposed. She felt powerful.

He pulled her closer and kissed her belly. His lips were warm, and his touch set alight a flame that burned through her.

He lifted her off her feet and she sat on his lap, her knees spread as she straddled him.

He ran his right hand along her thigh, over her waist and her shoulder until his thumb came to rest on her jaw. It was warm and soft, his pressure gentle. He ran his thumb along the line of her jaw and then his thumb was replaced by his lips. He kissed her neck, her collarbone and the hollow at the base of her throat where her collarbones met.

His fingers blazed a trail across her body that his mouth followed. Down from her throat to her sternum, over her breast to her nipple. His fingers flicked over the nipple, already peaked and hard. His mouth followed, covering it, sucking, licking and tasting.

He flipped her onto her back, lying her on the bed.

Moonlight danced across the ocean, streaming through the uncurtained windows, and fell across the bed. Her skin shone in the pale light.

He opened a bedside drawer and retrieved a condom as Viktoria reached for his boxer shorts and pulled them from his waist.

He was lying beside her now, and his fingers were stroking the inside of her thigh. She parted her legs and his fingers slid inside her, into her warm, moist centre. His thumb rolled over her most sensitive spot, making her gasp. He kissed her breast, sucking at her nipple as his thumb teased her. She arched her back, pushing her hips and breasts towards him, wanting more, letting him take her to a peak of desire.

Still she wanted more. She needed more.

She rolled towards him and pushed him flat onto his back. She sat up and straddled his hips again. His erection rose between them, trapped between their groins. Viktoria reached for the condom, and her breasts hung above his face. He lifted his head, taking her breast into his mouth once more. She closed her eyes as she gave herself up to the sensations shooting through her as his tongue flicked over her nipple. Every part of her responded to his touch. Her body came alive under his fingers and his lips and her skin burned where their bodies met.

She lifted herself clear of Cam, pulling her breast from his lips as she opened the condom. Air flowed over her nipple, the cool temperature contrasting with the heat of his mouth as she rolled the condom onto him. Her fingers encircled his shaft as she smoothed out the sheath.

She placed her hands either side of his head and kept her eyes on his face as she lifted herself up and took him inside her. His eyelids closed and she watched him breathe in deeply as her flesh encased him, joining them together.

She filled herself with his length before lifting her weight from him and letting him take control. His thumbs were on the front of her hips, his fingers behind her pelvis as he guided her up and down, matching her rhythm to his thrusts, each movement bringing her closer to climax

She liked this position. She liked being able to watch him, she liked being able to see him getting closer and closer to release. His eyes were closed, his lips were parted, his breathing was rapid and shallow, his thrusts getting faster.

She spread her knees, letting him in deeper inside her until she had taken all of him. Her body was flooded with heat. Every nerve ending was crying out for his touch. 'Now, Cam. Now.'

He opened his eyes and his grey gaze locked with hers as he took her to the top of the peak.

Her body started to quiver, and she watched him as he too shuddered. He closed his eyes, threw his head back and thrust into her, claiming her as they climaxed together.

When they were spent, she lay on him, covering his body with hers. Their skin felt warm and flushed from their effort and they were both panting as he wrapped his arms around her back, holding her to him. She could feel his heart beating under her chest. She could feel it as its rhythm slowed, gradually returning to normal.

They lay in silence as Viktoria resisted the urge to drift off to sleep. She knew she should get out of bed, get ready to leave. She would have to arrange for the hotel car to pick her up soon, but she wanted to stay in Cam's bed for a little longer.

Not for the first time, she wished she could experience dating like a normal person. As Cam offered to fetch them both a drink and got out of bed she lay there and imagined what it would be like to be able to spend the night. To not have to check in with Brigitta. To not have someone having to know her whereabouts at all times.

Perhaps she should have told Cam who she was, she thought. Perhaps she should have explained herself to him. Maybe then it wouldn't seem so odd that she was almost running for the door. That she couldn't stay the night.

She rolled over and sat up and noticed a photo frame lying face down on the other bedside table. They must have knocked it over while they made love. She reached out to stand it back up, looking at the photograph out of curiosity.

It was a photo of Cam with his arm around a woman with dark hair. Viktoria initially thought it was Skye but, when she looked again, she realised it wasn't.

She felt slightly queasy, a sensation she recognised as fear and jealousy running through her veins and making her nauseous. She hadn't seen any other personal photographs or mementos on display in his house. Was this Gemma in the photo? Why was she in the only photograph in his house and why was it beside his bed? She must be important but why hadn't he mentioned her? And why was the photograph lying down? Was he hiding something?

Viktoria was sitting up in bed when Cam returned to his room. She was bare-chested but her golden hair fell over her shoulders. The sheet was tangled around her waist and she reminded him of a mermaid perched on a rock. She looked beautiful and he wished he could ask her to stay the night, but he knew that would invite questions from Skye in the morning. Questions he wasn't ready to answer.

He put the glasses of water on the bedside table and then noticed Viktoria was holding something. A photo frame. The picture of him with Gemma.

'What are you doing?' he asked, his tone more abrupt than he'd intended.

Viktoria looked up at him. Her blue eyes were wide in her face. 'Who is this?'

'Gemma.'

'Is Gemma your girlfriend?'

'No.' He took the photo from her and put it back on the table. He turned it away from the bed. 'My fiancée.'

'Mon Dieu!' Viktoria sat back, putting some space between them. 'You did not think to mention that you are engaged?'

'I *was* engaged. Gemma is dead.'

He was being harsh, but he had finally stopped thinking about Gemma constantly since he'd begun spending time with Viktoria and that knowledge made him feel guilty. He didn't deserve to forget. Gemma deserved to be remembered.

'Pardon,' she said as she glanced at the back of the frame.

Cam knew the photo had been lying down. He knew she must have picked it up out of curiosity and he wasn't sure if she was apologising for prying or for his loss.

'Was it recent?' she asked.

'Two years ago.'

'Two years?' She paused and he could almost see the wheels turning in her mind. 'Your incident was two years ago, yes?'

Cam nodded. He knew what she was asking. 'Gemma was in the chopper too.'

'She was with you? She was in the army also?'

Cam could see the hurt in her eyes, and he knew he had been unnecessarily abrasive. It wasn't Viktoria's fault that he felt guilty.

'She was a pilot,' he said as he tried to make amends. He couldn't fix things for Gemma, but he had no reason to hurt Viktoria in the process. She had done nothing wrong. 'I joined the army because of her. I wanted to be with her. But I got her killed.'

'How do you figure that?'

'Gemma was one of only a handful of female pilots in the army. She loved to fly, and it was a great job. It took her all over the world but it took her away from me so I joined the medical corps so we could be together.'

'That does not make the crash your fault.'

He sat on the edge of the bed as he replied. 'On the day of the incident Gemma was on a rostered day off—she wasn't supposed to be flying—but one of the other pilots was sick. Gemma volunteered to cover his shift. She knew someone had to do it. She had a strong sense of duty and she also loved to fly. She told me there wasn't much point in having a day off if I was working. She thought she might as well work too. She wasn't supposed to be in the chopper that day.'

'If you had not been working would she have flown anyway?'

'She was rostered off. I would have been able to convince her to spend the day with me. Someone else could have taken over the roster. She volunteered because of *me*. She was only there because of me.'

'You told me the chopper was shot down. You had nothing to do with that. It was not your fault and I cannot imagine it was Gemma's either.'

'There was speculation that she was flying too high. Choppers tend to fly low, to keep out of sight, below the radar. It seemed as though the defence force were blaming Gemma. But it shouldn't have mattered. She should have been able to fly at any height. We were a medevac unit, well-marked. There was no mistaking us.'

Cam was quiet after that. Those memories were obviously hurting him, but Viktoria didn't know how to make things better.

She had been worried that he hadn't got over Gemma and was having trouble moving on, but learning that Gemma was dead, had been dead for two years, made her even more concerned. He hadn't let go. Which made her wonder what he was doing with her.

His friends had told her Cam didn't date. Had that been a warning that she'd ignored? Was she just a fling?

She couldn't be upset about that. After all, that was all she'd wanted too—one last adventure before she got married. She hadn't meant to get so invested.

She needed to stop obsessing, she thought as she let herself into the penthouse, and just enjoy the next few days. She liked him—really liked him—but they had a few days together, not a future.

'Good morning.' Cam bent down and kissed his sister's cheek. The sun was only just over the horizon, but Skye was already sitting outside by the pool nursing a cup of tea. It was a glorious morning, blue sky and not a breath of wind. Sydney had turned on spectacular weather for the Legion's Games and today was looking to be no exception. 'You're up early.'

'It's hard to sleep in when I feel like I constantly need to go to the toilet. This baby's favourite position seems to be lying on my bladder.'

'You sure you really need a cup of tea as well?'

'I need something; I'm exhausted. I can't wait for this baby to arrive.'

'You know all first-time mothers say that and then they realise that a good night's sleep is just as impossible to get after the baby is born?'

'I know, people keep warning me, but it'll be nice to stop waddling and to be able to see my toes again.'

'You won't be looking at your toes once you're cuddling your baby.'

'Fair point.' Skye laughed. 'Now, why don't you make yourself useful and bring us some breakfast? I've cut up some fruit; it's in the fridge.'

Cam made himself a coffee and carried it back to the table on a tray with fruit, bowls and yoghurt.

'So you're in a good mood,' she said as he pushed the newspaper and Skye's tablet out of the way, making room for the tray.

He was in a good mood. He had enjoyed last night and even talking about Gemma hadn't dampened his spirits. It had felt good to tell Viktoria about her. The honesty made him feel less guilty. He enjoyed Viktoria's company and that was okay. It was nothing to apologise for

'Does it have anything to do with where you were last night?' Skye asked.

'Sorry, I forgot you were coming.'

'That's okay. I have a key. So…where were you? Are you going to give me the goss?'

'I was out with Viktoria.'

'You went out with her again?'

'Yes.' Cam hesitated. 'I thought you'd be pleased that I wanted to see someone more than once. That I'm moving forward.'

'I am,' Skye said as she speared a piece of mango with her fork. 'Is it serious?'

'Why would you ask that? I've only known her a few days.'

'You brought her to our house, Cam. You haven't introduced Dave and me to any girl in two years. Not since Gemma.'

Cam hadn't thought about Gemma constantly for several days but now that he was finally able to have a moment's peace from his thoughts, her name kept coming up. But he didn't feel quite the same intense emotion of guilt and shame.

'It's not serious.'

Viktoria was the first woman in two years that he'd wanted to spend time with but that didn't make it serious.

She was the first woman in two years

who had been able to distract him for long
enough to make him forget about what had
happened. She was different to Gemma.
Gemma was non-stop, hyperactive, a type
A personality. She had challenged him and
pushed him but never given him a moment's
peace. Since the incident all he wanted was
peace. He needed calm and Viktoria brought
the calm, but she was only in Australia for
another few days.

It wasn't serious. He figured he could
safely spend as much time with her as he
liked—as they both liked—because he
knew there was a limit and that suited him
perfectly. He wasn't ready to open himself
up to another serious relationship.

'Oh. Okay.'

'What does that tone mean?' Cam asked.

'Nothing. I'm just not sure if that's good
or bad.'

He frowned. 'Why?'

'Has she told you much about herself?'
Skye asked as she reached for her tablet.

'What's going on?' His sister's behaviour
was making him nervous.

'I just wondered how much you know
about her.'

'Why? What have you heard?'

'I haven't heard anything, but I've read

some things. Von Grasburg. That's her sur-name, correct?' Skye tapped on the screen.

'Yes.' His good mood was beginning to evaporate, replaced by doubts. What was Skye getting at? 'What's this all about?'

'I thought she looked familiar the other day, but it wasn't until after you left that the penny dropped.'

'What penny? You're not making any sense.'

'Did she tell you she is an internationally recognised horse rider? She's represented Berggrun in cross-country eventing and has won some major medals. That's why she looked familiar.'

Skye was horse-mad. Cam wasn't sur-prised that she recognised Viktoria, but he didn't see why that information was rele-vant. 'No, I didn't know that. What does that matter?'

'You know Berggrun is a principality, right?'

'Yes.' That he did know.

'Well, it was bugging me that she looked familiar, so I searched her on the internet, and it mentions her international eventing medals but those aren't the first articles that pops up about her. The first one that comes up is a link to the royal family of Berggrun. Apparently, her father is the Prince.' Skye paused. 'Viktoria is a princess.'

CHAPTER SEVEN

'DON'T BE RIDICULOUS. She's not a princess.'

'I beg to differ.'

'She can't be.'

'She is.' Skye turned her tablet around so the screen was facing Cam.

There were links to articles about the royal family of Berggrun, but it was the photographs that caught his eye. Official photographs of the Prince and Princess and their three adult children. Two sons and a daughter. Despite the formal style of the picture and the outfits and the tiaras on the Princesses' heads, there was no mistaking Viktoria.

Skye was right. Cam couldn't deny it and, seeing the evidence, other things began to make more sense. Viktoria's driver, her accommodation in the hotel's penthouse suite, all the charity events she attended, even working for Prince Alfred. But there was one thing that didn't make sense. 'Why wouldn't she have told me?'

'I don't know—you'd have to ask her that—but I thought you should know before you did something stupid.'

'Like what?'

'Like take her to dinner, sleep with her and then not call her again,' Skye said. 'You can't do that to a princess.'

Too late, he thought. It seemed as though he'd already done something stupid.

Cam was at the base early in order to make some changes to the day's arrangements. He had rostered himself on to staff the medical tent at the athletics stadium, but he knew he wasn't in the right headspace to cope with what could potentially be a frantic day. He made some phone calls and swapped duties with one of the other doctors, which allowed him to remain on the base, supervising the medical staff who were in attendance for the archery. He assumed two things: one, that Viktoria would most likely be attending the high-profile athletics events and two, that there would be fewer injuries at the archery, which would give him time to think.

He needed to work out what he was going to do.

Should he pretend he didn't know who she was and continue on as before? No. He couldn't do that.

So what option did that leave him? To confront her and ask her why she hadn't told him that she was royalty? But then what?

He couldn't avoid her indefinitely and he couldn't stay angry at her either. He was upset with himself for opening up to her, for sharing his feelings, only to find out there was so much she hadn't shared with him, but he knew he would have to speak to her at some point; she deserved a chance to explain and he wanted answers. But he wanted to be on the front foot for that discussion. He knew he would see her tonight at the barbecue for the athletes that was being hosted by Prince Alfred. He couldn't skip that event, so he needed to spend some time today figuring out what to say.

Viktoria was convinced that Cam was avoiding her. He had told her he would see her at the athletics stadium today, but she hadn't seen him there and had later found out that he was at the archery. And now, even though she'd seen him at the barbecue, he hadn't come near her.

She had tried several times to speak to

him but every time she spotted him in the crowd he had moved elsewhere by the time she got near. He was definitely avoiding her, and she needed to know why.

She was talking to Mark, congratulating him on winning a medal in archery, when she saw Cam watching her. This was her chance to find out if there was a problem. She pinned him with her gaze, challenging him to walk away, but this time he didn't move.

'Are you avoiding me?' She waited for him to deny it, to reassure her, but he was silent, confirming her fears. 'Is this about Gemma?' she asked.

'Gemma?'

She had only come up with one reason why he would be avoiding her, and it was all to do with the photo she had seen of him with Gemma—the fact that he'd had a fiancée. That they hadn't broken up through choice but because she had died. She was convinced he felt he had made a mistake bringing her to his house.

'I wondered if you were sorry that you took me home. If you felt I was intruding on Gemma's memory.'

'No. It's not about Gemma. And she never saw my house. I bought it after the incident.'

'So, what is the matter?'

She saw him take in their surroundings. Everywhere they looked were soldiers and their families. 'Not here. Let's go somewhere quieter.'

He led her around to the side of the gym, towards the car park, where there was less chance of their conversation being overheard. 'When were you planning on telling me?' he asked once they were alone.

'Telling you what?'

'That you're a princess.'

She had thought she had done something to upset him, or that he regretted telling her about Gemma. That their conversation last night had brought back memories that had been too much for him to handle. That he'd felt guilty about taking her home. As if perhaps he felt he was cheating on Gemma, or at least on her memory.

She had thought a lot of things, but she hadn't suspected that he knew who she really was.

She was floored. Freddie had never betrayed her trust before. He'd always had her back. She knew he'd thought her unwise to keep her identity from Cam but she had never anticipated that he'd divulge her secret. And Cam was obviously upset.

Her stomach dropped and her heart was racing. How much damage had Freddie done?

'Freddie told you?'

'Freddie? Who the hell is Freddie?'

Viktoria frowned. 'Prince Alfred. My cousin.'

'Your cousin?'

Viktoria nodded. 'You didn't know?'

'No.'

'How did you find out then?' She knew as she spoke that she sounded guilty. She sounded as if she'd been trying to hide the fact that she was royalty. Which she had. But for good reason. At least from her point of view, but, if the expression on Cam's face was any indication, it looked as though he disagreed.

'Skye told me. She thought she recognised you. It turns out she did, from cross-country eventing, but she found more than she'd bargained for. But she didn't tell me you're related to Prince Alfred.'

'What does it matter?'

'What does it *matter*? You're a *princess*! There must be some sort of protocol, some rules, for dating a princess. I'm sure it's not right to sleep with a princess on a second date. I never would have done that if I'd known who you are.'

'And that is exactly why I did not tell you. I just wanted to be treated like a normal person. I did not think you needed to know I am a princess. I like you and I wanted to know that you liked me, Viktoria. Not me, the princess.'

'I don't appreciate being lied to.'

'I never lied to you.'

'Maybe not, but you didn't tell me the truth either,' he said as he walked away.

She watched him go. She couldn't make him stay and she didn't know what else to say.

She could feel tears threatening. She shouldn't be upset. She shouldn't let him get to her, but it was too late. It hurt.

It shouldn't matter. It was never going to be a long-term possibility, but it hurt her more than she expected to be cast aside like that.

She really liked him. She enjoyed his company. He was intelligent, handsome, great in bed. A little moody and guarded, but she had seen glimpses of what he would be like if he would let his guard down, enjoy himself, and she'd been looking forward to the next week.

Would she be able to make it up to him? Would he calm down, see reason? Would she be able to explain herself to him—to make him understand why it was important to her to keep that side of her life private—or would he walk away without a backward glance?

Freddie had been right. She should have told him who she was, but all that would have done was speed up the inevitable.

He didn't want to date a princess.

She ducked into the gym and headed for the female toilets. She needed a moment to compose herself; she didn't want anyone to see her cry.

She'd thought not telling him she was a princess was the right thing to do. She'd thought it didn't matter, but she was wrong. And he was right. She had lied by omission.

She would apologise. That was the right thing to do.

She took several deep breaths and blew her nose. She touched up her make-up, grateful that Brigitta had taught her a few tricks, and steeled herself to go back outside. To find him. To apologise.

She opened the door and almost collided with a woman coming the other way.

'*Pardon!*'

The woman had a dog by her side and Viktoria realised it was Fiona with Leroy.

'*Bonjour*, Fiona. How are you?'

Fiona looked up at the sound of her name, but Viktoria could see that she didn't recognise her immediately. 'It is me, Viktoria. We met in the gymnasium the other day.'

'Oh, yes. Hi.'

Fiona looked a little pale, but her skin had a sheen that looked like she'd been sweating. She had one hand on Leroy's head and Viktoria got the sense that the dog was anchoring Fiona rather than Fiona controlling the dog.

'Are you all right?' she asked.

'I just needed to catch my breath. The crowd is bigger than I expected. I just need a quiet minute.'

Fiona lifted her other hand and steadied herself against the door jamb, but Viktoria could see her hand was shaking. Viktoria was concerned; Fiona didn't look alright.

Viktoria frowned as Leroy began whining.

Fiona didn't seem to notice the dog's distress, which concerned Viktoria even more. 'You should sit down and I will get you a drink of water,' she offered. She was reluctant to leave her alone, but she didn't know what to do. There was a chair in the vestibule just outside the bathroom door and Viktoria led Fiona to it. 'I will not be long,' she said as she went to find a water cooler.

She had taken less than three steps when Leroy's whining morphed into frantic barking. Alarmed, Viktoria turned around and saw Fiona collapsed on the tiled floor. She was shaking uncontrollably, and Viktoria recognised the signs of a seizure.

She knew what was happening, but she wasn't sure what to do. She needed to get help, but was it safe to leave her?

She moved the chair, concerned that Fiona would hit her head, before realising that she could still hit her head on the wall. Leroy was still barking furiously. Maybe someone would hear him and come to investigate, but she couldn't take that chance. She needed to get help. She didn't want to be responsible for Fiona. This was out of her area of expertise.

She knew the bathroom was empty. She had to go and find someone.

She left Fiona with Leroy. She knew the dog wouldn't leave Fiona's side.

She ran outside and scanned the crowd, looking for assistance. Looking for Cam.

He hadn't got far. He was only a few metres away, talking to Sean and Lisa.

'Campbell! *Vite! Vite!*'

Cam turned at the sound of her voice and Viktoria beckoned to him, waving her arm frantically. Fiona's seizure had distracted her from her own problems and all she felt was relief at seeing Cam. Their issues were pushed to the back of her mind; she had far more pressing concerns.

Cam took a second or two before he started moving towards her and for a moment she wondered if he would ignore her.

But he didn't. He couldn't, she supposed. It was obvious something wasn't right.

He hurried towards her, but she couldn't wait. She ran to meet him. *'Vite, vite,'* she said as she grabbed his hand. 'Hurry. Fiona is having some sort of a seizure.' She pulled him along with her, back to the gymnasium.

'Fiona?'

Viktoria didn't know her last name. She'd assumed Cam knew everyone. 'She is competing in the rowing event. She has a service dog, Leroy,' she said, giving him the only other identifying information she knew.

She could still hear Leroy barking as they entered the gym but as she pushed open the door into the ladies' toilets and the dog saw them he quietened down, emitting a soft whine instead. He was pacing around Fiona, who was still convulsing on the hard floor.

Cam brushed past Viktoria. She saw him check the time on his watch as he pulled his phone from his pocket. He swiped the password, dialled a number and handed it to her. 'There's an ambulance stationed on the base for the Games; I've just dialled them. When they answer, put them on speaker for me. Can you do that?' he asked as he thrust the phone at her and knelt on the floor.

Viktoria nodded as she took the phone. She held it to her ear as she watched Cam get to work.

He unbuttoned his shirt and ripped it off, stripping down to the khaki T-shirt that moulded to his chest and arms. He bundled his shirt up and put it under Fiona's head, protecting her from the cold, hard, unforgiving tiles.

He talked in a low, quiet voice. Viktoria wasn't sure if he was talking to Fiona or the dog, but the dog calmed down. He stopped pacing and stood at Cam's shoulder. He seemed to sense that Cam was trying to help.

Viktoria put the phone on speaker as the call was answered. She quickly explained what had happened before holding the phone towards Cam.

He sat back on his heels, keeping one eye on his watch as he spoke to the paramedics.

'This is Dr Cam Hamilton. I'm with a female soldier who is having a seizure. We're in the women's toilets at the back of the gym.'

'She sustained a serious head injury a year ago. No history of seizures that I know of, but this one has been going for several minutes.'

'What do we do now?' Viktoria asked when Cam finished his phone conversation.

'We wait for the ambulance. There's nothing else we can do.'

'And when they come?'

'She'll need to go to hospital. We'll need to run some tests to see if we can determine the cause of the seizure.'

'I don't know how you do this. This constant surge of adrenalin. Of drama.'

'It's not so dramatic when you're trained to deal with it.'

The paramedics arrived as Fiona's seizure finally abated. Within minutes they had loaded her onto a stretcher and into the ambulance. Cam had offered to take Leroy and follow them to the hospital. Viktoria wasn't sure if that was really in his job description or whether it just gave him an excuse to get away from her.

She didn't know and she wasn't about to ask.

Viktoria had spent the morning watching the road cycling event. The course was spectacular; it began and ended at the Opera House but wound its way around the harbour and through the Botanic Gardens, which gave the spectators plenty of vantage points from which to watch the race. A large number of them had spread picnic blankets on the lawns of the gardens and were sitting in the spring sunshine cheering the cyclists on as they rode past.

Viktoria had been present at the start, taking photographs to upload to the social media pages, and while she'd kept an eye out for Cam, she'd stayed clear of the medical tent. She wasn't sure if he was even working at the cycling today and, while she wanted to see him, she didn't want to talk to him. She was afraid of what he might say.

She tried to focus on her job, but it was difficult to be enthusiastic when her brain was crowded with thoughts of Cam.

She still needed to apologise.

She wondered if he'd forgive her.

At the end of the day's events, to distract herself from spending all her time thinking about Campbell and what she could have—or should have—done differently, Viktoria called in to the hospital to visit Fiona.

She was relieved, and a little surprised, to find her in her room looking perfectly well.

'You are all right?' she asked.

'Apparently so,' Fiona said.

'Do you remember what happened?'

'Not really. I was told I was lucky you were there, though. You made sure I got immediate attention, so thank you.'

'I am glad I was able to be useful. Have you had a seizure before?'

'No. Never.'

'Do you know what caused it?'

Fiona shook her head. 'I had some scans done today. The doctors think that when I had the accident in the Middle East I suffered a traumatic brain injury along with multiple fractures. The brain damage can manifest as seizures.'

'What will happen now?'

'I think the doctors will just monitor me. If it happens again or frequently, I might need medication but I'm already on several.'

'And how are you feeling?'

'I'm tired and I feel like I've got a massive hangover, but the doctors assure me that is normal,' she said.

The door opened and one of the nurses came in and ushered Viktoria out with a brisk instruction. 'The patient needs to rest.'

'Bien sûr.'

Viktoria said goodbye to Fiona and headed for the lift. The doors opened and Cam stepped out, surprising her. She felt her knees wobble. She put her hand out, reaching for the wall to steady herself. 'Campbell! Are you here to see Fiona?'

'Yes.'

'Do you have a minute?' Maybe this was her chance.

'Not really.' His eyes were guarded.

'Please. It is important,' she said, knowing she might not get another opportunity to apologise.

He sighed and took a step forward and she thought he was going to continue walking past her, but he inclined his head and said, 'Follow me.' He pushed open a door to a small lounge, which Viktoria realised was a waiting area for families of patients. She could only imagine the sorts of things they'd been told inside these four walls.

'What is it?' he asked as she followed him inside.

'I owe you an apology.'

'I don't need an apology. I need an explanation,' he said as he closed the door behind them. 'Why didn't you tell me who you are?'

'I just wanted a chance to be anonymous. To be ordinary. All my life, people have wanted a part of me. They are fascinated by royalty, by the fame and fortune they assume is associated with it. I have never known who has wanted to get to know me and who has wanted to know the Princess. I am never sure who to trust.'

'I'm not interested in fame and fortune.'

'And this wasn't about keeping a secret from you; I was keeping it from everyone.'

'I didn't think I was just anyone.'

'You are right. I should have told you, but I did not want it to change the way you felt about me. I wanted you to get to know the real me. I wanted you to see me. I wanted you to lo…to like me without knowing that I am a princess.'

'You can't pretend not to be who you are. There are two sides to you. You can't separate them.'

'I wanted some freedom to just be me,

Viktoria. Being a princess is only a title. I just wanted to be the same as everyone else.'

'But, at the end of the day, you're not, are you?'

'I am still me.'

'And who is that?'

She wasn't sure any more. She had thought she'd enjoy pretending to be a commoner and, at the end of the adventure, she'd be ready to return home, back to the life of a princess. Back to her duty. She had made a promise to her parents, but she'd never imagined that she'd want to change her mind. That she might not want to return.

But what was the alternative? Could she seriously imagine staying in Australia? Giving up everything she knew?

She didn't know what to tell him, so she said nothing.

'You talk about trust,' Cam said, 'yet you didn't trust me enough to tell me who you are. You should have been honest with me. You should have trusted me like I trusted you. I confided in you, but you couldn't confide in me. Or you chose not to. I have told you things about myself that no one else knows and you've told me half-truths.'

'*Non!* Everything I have told you about myself is true. I am a daughter, a sister, an aunt. I have a marketing degree and I do spend my time at charity events and handing out trophies. I have not lied to you.'

'But you haven't been completely honest either.'

'No. But I wanted to forget I was a princess. With you I felt like Viktoria and that was what I wanted. You made me happy. I hoped I was making you happy too.'

'I don't deserve to be happy.'

CHAPTER EIGHT

'Everyone deserves to be happy,' Viktoria told him.

But Cam disagreed. 'No. Not me. I don't get to be happy.'

'Why not?'

'Why should I get to be happy? When Gemma is dead.'

'I realise I did not know her, but I cannot imagine she would not want you to be happy. The incident was not your fault. You didn't fire the missile. Whoever did that is the one who killed her. Who almost killed you.'

'But if it wasn't for me, she wouldn't have been there.'

'That was not your decision. That was hers. That was her job. You told me she felt it was her duty. I know what that is like and I am sure you do too. You cannot blame yourself for that.'

'Maybe not, but I should have saved her.

Even if I couldn't have stopped her from flying, I was there and I should have saved her. And I couldn't. I'm a doctor. It's my job to save lives. And I let her die.'

'What about the other people who were in the chopper with you? Do you feel the same responsibility for them?'

'No.'

As a doctor, Cam knew that there was nothing he could have done for them. They'd most likely been dead before they'd hit the ground and, with no functioning equipment and with his extensive injuries, he couldn't have helped them.

'Well, is it not the same for Gemma?'

'No.' He shook his head. 'My Hippocratic Oath is to do no harm. That's different from promising to be there for her always. We were a couple, we were engaged. I promised to protect her—to look after her—and I let her down.'

'Cam, you have to forgive yourself. You have to give yourself permission to move on. You are living a half-life, afraid to let people in. That is no way to live. I should know. It is rare that I am able to be my true self. That is one of the things I have loved about spending time with you, and the reason I did not tell you everything about me.

I wanted to be free to live my life, and you should do the same.'

She was most likely right but that didn't mean he was ready to change his ways. Because of Gemma, he was prepared to connect physically with people but not emotionally. His heart was hardened now. He wasn't afraid he'd get hurt, he wasn't afraid of letting people in; he was afraid of letting people down.

'Your guilt is stopping you from being happy,' she said. 'It is not my fault I am a princess. It is not your fault Gemma died. We can choose to live our lives the best we can, or we can choose to give up. It was Gemma's choice to fly that day. It was her duty. You are not to blame.'

He knew Viktoria was right. Gemma had been all about her duty. He supposed Viktoria was the same.

'I understand you have suffered trauma and a terrible loss,' she continued, 'but that does not mean you cannot care about people. I have seen you with your sister, your friends, with Rex. I have heard you talk about your work. I know you care about these people, these things—do you think you could care about me?'

He did care about her, but he didn't want

to. That was his dilemma. He knew Viktoria's sense of duty would mean the end of their relationship. He knew her sense of duty would take her away from him, just as Gemma's had done. And there was nothing he could do about it. He couldn't be a part of her life. He wasn't right for her; she didn't need someone damaged, someone disillusioned. She needed someone who could fit into her royal life, and he knew for certain that wasn't him. He didn't know how to be a royal. And she wasn't asking him to try. She knew as well as he did they didn't have a future, that he wasn't suitable.

Their relationship was never going to last. It was always going to end. It was probably better that it ended now.

'I have to go,' he said. He didn't want to go but he couldn't stay either.

Viktoria was the first person he had felt a connection to since Gemma died, but that didn't mean they could make it work.

Cam thanked the waiter as he put a plate of seared tuna in front of him.

He was one of thirty guests seated around a table at a dinner hosted by Prince Alfred. He had invited them to dinner in a private dining room in one of Sydney's five-star restaurants as a personal thank you to the Australian members of the Legion's Games Committee. There were two days of competition remaining and, while Cam appreciated the invitation, he was attending under sufferance and at Doug's insistence.

Viktoria was seated at the other end of the table, diagonally opposite him. He could see her but he couldn't have a conversation with her. He hadn't spoken to her since he'd bumped into her at the hospital. He didn't know what to say.

She looked amazing. But her eyes looked sad.

Had he done that to her?

Had he been foolish?

Should he have ignored the fact that she was a princess? Would there really have been any harm in continuing to see her for a few more days?

Maybe no harm but also no point. She couldn't leave her life. She had a duty. And what could he possibly offer her?

He couldn't fit in to her world.

She'd said they could be happy together, but he'd meant it when he said he didn't deserve to be happy.

He told himself it had never been serious,

but that didn't explain why he still felt distraught at the idea that it was over.

He sighed and cut into his tuna. It looked superb and he was sure it was delicious, but he had no appetite. Prince Alfred was seated three chairs away and Cam noticed he didn't seem to be enjoying his dinner either.

A sheen of perspiration shone on the Prince's forehead.

'Are you all right, Your Highness?'

The Prince had his hand pressed to his stomach, his fingers probing. 'I've had a bit of abdominal pain today. I think I might have strained a muscle when I did that rowing challenge yesterday.'

Viktoria had organised for Prince Alfred to race against some of the rowers as a publicity and morale-boosting exercise.

Cam thought his explanation sounded plausible until he saw the Prince wince and gasp with pain as all the colour drained from his face. That looked far too painful to be a pulled muscle. The Prince's fingers had been pressing over the right side of his stomach and Cam had a suspicion that he was suffering from something more sinister than a muscle strain.

'Would you mind if I took a look, Your Highness? Just in case it's not muscular.'

Cam was aware by now that they had the attention of most of the table. There was a small bar area adjacent the private dining room where they had gathered for predinner drinks and he recalled seeing a few small couches in that space. 'Perhaps we could go to the room next door?'

Beads of sweat broke out on the Prince's forehead as he stood. He winced when he took a step, putting his weight on his right foot.

Doug had left his seat and was beside Cam. 'Can I help? What do you need?'

'Just keep everyone in here for now. I'll let you know,' Cam replied as he put one hand under the Prince's elbow to support some of his weight without making it look like the Prince was in need of his assistance.

Cam was aware that Viktoria was standing too. She ignored Doug's instructions and followed them out into the small bar area.

She stood behind Cam as he got the Prince to lie on the sofa. Cam couldn't see her, she wasn't in his way but she was in his head. He could smell her perfume and he knew the scent of gardenias would always remind him of her.

He tried to block her presence out so he could concentrate on examining the Prince.

He placed the back of one hand on the Prince's forehead, feeling for a temperature, although he could tell by looking at him that he was feverish.

'You have pain when you're walking?'

The Prince nodded.

'Any nausea?'

Another nod.

'I'm just going to press on your stomach,' Cam said. 'Is that okay?'

A third nod. The Prince was clammy, pale and in obvious distress. Cam pressed his fingers gently over the Prince's abdomen, over the lower right quadrant. As he released the pressure the Prince grimaced and complained.

Cam turned to Viktoria. 'Do you think you could ask Doug to come out here?'

'What is wrong?' Viktoria asked.

Cam turned back to the Prince, giving him his suspected diagnosis. 'I take it you have never had your appendix removed?'

The Prince shook his head.

'I think you have appendicitis. I am going to call an ambulance and take you to hospital. I think we need to investigate this.' Cam pulled his phone from his pocket as Viktoria went to fetch Doug. He dialled the ambulance; he'd get Doug to explain what had happened to the Prince's guests. He had other priorities.

'Right now?' The Prince could barely get the words out.

'Yes. I don't want to wait. If your appendix bursts, you'll be in a world of trouble. It's too big a risk.' Cam wasn't about to take a chance with a royal life.

Cam and Viktoria followed the ambulance to North Sydney Hospital. Cam made some phone calls on the way, calling in favours, getting the best surgeons on the job.

The Prince was whisked away on arrival, leaving Cam and Viktoria waiting for news.

It was not as straightforward as they had hoped.

Appendicitis was confirmed but while he was being prepped for Theatre his appendix burst, meaning he needed open abdominal surgery instead of the less invasive laparoscopic procedure. A burst appendix could be life-threatening.

'What do I tell Auntie Ingrid?'

'Who?'

'Fred's mother.'

'Tell her he has excellent surgeons operating on him and that you'll call with an update as soon as he is out of Theatre.'

'Will you wait with me?'

'Yes.' He had no intention of leaving her to wait on her own. 'Tell me about your family,' he said, hoping to distract her. 'You have spent a lot of time with your cousins?'

Viktoria nodded. 'We spent our holidays together every year. We would go skiing and usually spent summer together as well. My cousins are similar ages to my brothers and me. Freddie and I are the babies but he is eighteen months older than me. He has always been protective of me.'

'And now? You're still close, obviously.'

'We are. I think it is because it was always hard to know who to trust. To know who wanted to be friends because of the family we were born into rather than because of who we are. We could trust each other. We relied on each other. He will be okay, *oui*?'

'He's in the best place, in the best hands.'

'How long will he be in hospital?'

'A couple of days, I should think. It will be important to make sure there is no infection.'

'But there are only two days left of the Games.'

'I think it's safe to say he will miss the rest.'

She went quiet.

'He'll be fine.'

'I know. I believe you. I was just thinking about all the things Freddie is scheduled to do over the next two days. Handing out the medals, making a speech at the closing ceremony.'

'Someone else will have to take over.'

'I know,' she sighed.

'Will that be you?'

'Most likely. It is what I do. I cannot seem to get away from handing out trophies and making speeches. I have enjoyed my anonymity, but I always knew it would not last. But I had hoped I could make it through my last two days here.' She shrugged.

'Two days?' He hadn't actually confirmed exactly when she was leaving. He hadn't wanted to think about it.

'*Oui.* I leave the day after the Games.'

'So soon?'

She nodded. 'I have to go home. My father has been Prince for twenty-five years. There are big celebrations planned, starting in five days. I have to be there. You could come with me?'

'To Berggrun?'

She nodded.

'I don't think so.'

'Why not?'

'I don't think that's a world I'd be comfortable in.'

'You cannot make that decision without experiencing it.'

He shook his head. Viktoria had a duty and he didn't begrudge that but, like Gemma, her duty was to more than her job. It was to her country.

He couldn't compete with that.

CHAPTER NINE

VIKTORIA WAS BACK at the hospital first thing the following morning. She was beginning to feel as if she was seeing more of Sydney's hospitals than anything else. But the surgeon was confident that Freddie would be fine and that was the important thing, she reminded herself as she pushed open the door to his room.

'*Bonjour!* How are you feeling today? Good?'

'I wouldn't say "good". I'm still really sore but apparently that is now from the surgery, so I suppose that's a positive.'

'And when can you get out of here?'

'Not until tomorrow at the earliest. I still have a slight temperature and the doctors want to make sure there is no infection. Which means I have a favour to ask you.'

Viktoria knew what was coming. 'You want me to hand out the medals?'

'Yes. But I also might need you to give my closing ceremony speech.'

'But that is not until tomorrow!'

'I know. But, just as a precaution, could you familiarise yourself with it?'

Viktoria nodded. 'If you will be in hospital until tomorrow will you be allowed to fly the day after that?' Freddie was supposed to be leaving with her. He was also expected at her father's celebrations.

'No. I'll have to delay my trip by a couple of days.'

'You cannot fly back with me?'

'No. Can you stay longer? It might give you a chance to sort things out with Campbell.'

Viktoria had told Freddie the details of her latest woes. To his credit he hadn't reminded her that he'd warned her the decision to keep her identity a secret might not be the wisest choice and she knew he was trying to be supportive.

She shook her head. 'I promised my parents I would be home in time for the preparations for the celebrations. I need to go. Plus, there is nothing to sort out. It was never going to be anything more than a holiday romance.'

She had been trying to convince herself

of that, but she couldn't let go of the feeling that it could have been more. But that was obviously only her perception. Cam wanted nothing to do with her.

'I'm sorry, Viktoria.'

'It is okay. I think I was kidding myself. Thinking we could have a proper relationship. It is just that I felt I could be my true self with him. Not a royal. Just Viktoria.'

'But at some point he had to know the truth.'

'I know,' she sighed. 'I just wish he could see past that.'

'Are you sure there's no way of making it work?'

'I am sure. Our timing is not right. He is not ready. And I cannot wait for him to *be* ready. That may never happen, and I do not have the luxury of time.'

'Is he worth waiting for? Do you think he could be the one?'

Was it possible? Could it be?

'I do not know. If I am honest there are so many hurdles. He will not let go of his guilt and I cannot let go of who I am. I cannot let go of my duty. You know my parents are expecting to announce my engagement on my return.'

'Would you give it up for him if he asked you to?'

'If he was the person I want him to be he would not ask me to.'

But she knew that if he told her he loved her and asked her to stay she would do everything in her power to make it happen. She felt as if she was the person she wanted to be when they were together. She felt they were meant to be.

But would she be prepared to sacrifice her title for him? She knew it was unfair of her to expect him to make sacrifices for her if she wasn't prepared to do the same.

It was complicated.

She'd thought love would be simple.

Somehow Viktoria had made it through the final day. The past two days had passed in a blur of exhaustion and despair but there was now only one final event—the four by fifty-metre swimming relay. She had one more medal presentation to get through before the closing ceremony tonight and then tomorrow she would be on a plane, going home to a life she wasn't sure she wanted.

Her life felt totally out of control. Nothing was going the way she wanted. Three weeks ago, she had never set foot in Australia and now she didn't want to leave. She could imagine a future here, with Cam. She could imagine herself with a real job, perhaps working with the veterans and therapy horses. But it was all a fantasy. There was no way she could stay.

She had fallen in love with a man who didn't want her and now she had to go home to a life that she didn't want——a life that was being planned for her. She'd mucked that up too, but she couldn't see a way out of it. Her title and her duty were a burden she had to bear.

She made her way back to her seat after the medal presentation as the next lot of competitors came out onto the pool deck. The teams were announced over the loudspeaker and she was only half listening, lost in her own thoughts, when she bumped into Mark.

'Mark! Why are you not with your team?'

'I've decided not to swim. My shoulder is still sore, and I don't want to let my team down.'

'But it is a relay! What will they do without you?'

'We have a reserve. Campbell is swimming.'

'Campbell!' Just the mention of his name

made her heart race. 'Really?' she asked as she saw Skye walking towards her.

'Skye! Hello.' What was she doing there? There could be only one reason. 'Did you know Cam was swimming?'

'Of course; he called to tell me.' Skye frowned. 'Surely you knew?'

Viktoria shook her head as they kept walking towards the tiered seats. She felt as if she was the only one who was out of the loop. '*Non.* We have not been speaking. He is upset with me.'

'What? Why not? What's happened?'

'He is unhappy with me. He thought I was keeping something from him. I cannot blame him—I was. But I had my reasons.'

She wondered what he would say if he found out she had kept more than her royal connections from him. What would he say if he knew she would be returning home to choose a fiancé?

They took their seats as the teams were being introduced and Viktoria thought the crowd noise might prevent Skye from asking further questions but she was not deterred. At least the volume of voices would make it difficult for anyone else to overhear Viktoria's summary of the past few days as she explained to Skye what had happened.

She figured it didn't matter if Skye knew her story; it was likely that Cam would tell his sister what had happened at some point.

Viktoria finished bringing Skye up-to-date just as the Australians completed the third leg of the relay. Cam was swimming the final leg and the Americans were leading as he dived in. They were three metres ahead. He had fifty metres in which to catch them.

The British swimmer dived in seconds after Cam. The race was close. The crowd was deafening.

Viktoria wished she could cheer and scream from the stands along with the crowd but since she had taken over Freddie's duties everyone knew she was a princess, which meant she had to behave with decorum. She had duties and obligations to fulfil; she couldn't wear her heart on her sleeve, not when she and Cam were not officially a couple.

Her heart was pounding in her chest. She felt as if she was swimming alongside Cam.

He was making ground, but the end of the pool was only a few metres away. Would he run out of time?

He drew level.

There were two more strokes and they

seemed to touch the wall simultaneously, Cam and the American.

Everyone looked to the screen to see the result.

Cam had touched point zero one of a second in front of the American. The Australians had won. The crowd erupted and Viktoria couldn't keep the smile off her face. She turned and hugged Skye as the crowd cheered.

Viktoria made her way down to the pool deck, preparing to hand out the final round of medals in Freddie's place. She managed to say the right things and to congratulate the third placed British swimmers and the American silver medallists but the closer she got to the Australians the more nervous she became. Their team was lined up in the order that they swam so Cam was the final competitor to get his medal. Her hands were shaking as she hung the medal around his neck.

She kissed him on both cheeks as she wondered if that would be the last time she would do that.

'Congratulations,' she said as she stepped back. She needed some space; she needed some room to clear her head. 'You swam a fantastic race. When did you know you were swimming?'

'Only this morning,' he replied.

She was hurt that he hadn't told her. But, then again, everything hurt at the moment and saying goodbye was going to hurt most of all.

Hordes of people, family and friends, waited to congratulate the relay team as they emerged from the changing rooms after the medal ceremony. Cam knew he should be pleased. He'd swum well, he hadn't let anyone down and they had won. They were victorious. But once again life had lost its lustre; he could feel no pleasure.

He missed Viktoria.

But there was nothing he could do about that.

He searched the faces of the crowd, knowing he was hoping to see her, but she was nowhere to be found. Instead he saw Skye making her way towards him. She was frowning. He recognised that expression and knew she was about to reprimand him about something as only an older sister could. She certainly didn't look as if she was about to congratulate him on his race.

'What's going on with you and Viktoria?'

'What do you mean?'

'She just told me that you aren't speaking to her because of who she is.'

Cam led Skye away from the crowd, out of earshot. He was *not* going to have this conversation where anyone could hear them. 'That's not exactly true. I am speaking to her; I'm just distancing myself.'

'Why? Because she is a princess?'

'Among other things.'

'I thought you liked her?'

'I do, but it was never going to be serious. She was always going to leave.'

'You don't have to let her go.'

'I do. She's a *princess*. She has duties and obligations that I can't compete with. She's not going to give those up for me and I wouldn't ask her to.' He didn't like the idea that he was going to lose her. He'd lost Gemma because of a sense of duty and he was going to lose Viktoria too, but he couldn't stand in her way.

He understood her duty and he didn't begrudge her, but he knew he couldn't expect her to choose him over the throne. He thought he was doing the right thing by letting her go. Her sense of duty would always come first, and he didn't want her to feel torn between him and her role as a princess, but he also didn't want to play second fiddle. He couldn't see how they could make it work. He didn't know if she would want to try.

Meeting Viktoria had shown him that he was lonely. She had shown him what was missing from his life and he realised now he wanted another meaningful relationship, he was ready, but it was ridiculous to think that Viktoria was the woman for him. He'd only known her for two weeks.

He was going to miss her, but he'd get over her. But the more time he spent with her the harder that would be and the more it would hurt when she left.

And it didn't matter what he thought or what Skye thought; ultimately the decision was Viktoria's.

'She's leaving, Skye. She's not going to choose me.'

Viktoria took a deep breath as she stood up in front of one thousand athletes and their families and prepared to give Freddie's speech at the closing ceremony.

'Most of you will know by now that Prince Alfred had emergency surgery two days ago for a burst appendix.' The emergency had been heavily covered in the media. 'He is extremely disappointed that he is unable to be here tonight to share in the celebrations of what have been an amazing event, but he has entrusted me to deliver his message to you all.

'I want to commend all the athletes for your commitment, service and sacrifice for your countries. You have been brave in battle and brave also in the face of adversity, injury and illness to compete in these Games. If you have been watching these Games and thinking, *I could never do this*, know that you can. Every one of this year's competitors is willing to be a mentor to the next competitor, the next survivor. Be brave. Reach out. Together, anything is possible.

'Hopefully, these Games challenged your bodies, your minds and restored your spirit. Your resilience. Your efforts have captured the hearts not only of the Australian public but of the world. You should be proud of what you have achieved. Hold your heads high, continue to set goals and enjoy your lives, your friends and your families.

'I want to congratulate not just the athletes but also the families for your determination, courage and pride. Together, you've shown everyone what is possible. I am so proud to be associated with these Games and I will see you again next year in Vancouver.'

Viktoria paused while the crowd applauded Freddie's words before adding her own.

'And now I would also like to add my congratulations and my thanks to all of you. I feel very privileged that I got to meet so many of you over the past few days and that you shared your stories with me. Thank you for letting me be a part of these Games. Your friendships have inspired me and I hope that by sharing your stories with the world I have been able to inspire others to strive to achieve, to persevere and to embrace opportunities. To embrace life. To dig deep. To support each other and to reach out.

'Set goals and you can achieve something amazing. Many of you started with something simple, a goal to get out of bed in the morning, have a shower, walk around the block, talk to someone in the supermarket, to connect with people, and then you set the bar higher and that eventually brought you here, to the Games. Congratulations—you should all be so proud of your efforts.'

She had been aware of Cam standing just to the left of the stage throughout her speech. She'd tried to block him out, tried to avoid looking in his direction, knowing it would be difficult to hold her emotions in check and impossible to speak if she made eye contact with him but at the end of her address she made her way down from the stage and sought him out. There was something she did need to say.

'Dr Hamilton, do you have a minute?'

She was going to be brave. She could do this.

'I wanted to say goodbye before I left.'

'You're leaving now?'

She was always going to leave. She had obligations and promises to keep but she was going to take some lessons from the Games.

'*Oui*. I have learnt a lot from this experience—mostly about myself—but I think I am stronger and more focused, which is not a bad thing. I am going to use my position as a royal to make real change. I am not going to be content with presenting ribbons and trophies; I am going to get more involved with causes. If I am going to have a life of duty, I am going to make sure it is one I am proud of.

'But I wanted to thank you too, for everything. For making time for me. I realise I made some mistakes; I realise I am complicated, difficult even, and that my situation is unusual, but I enjoyed getting to know you and I will not forget you.'

She leant forward and kissed him on each cheek before turning around quickly and walking away before he could see her tears.

She wanted to have a public and private life. A purpose and a relationship.

She knew that the Viktoria she wanted to be had to co-exist with Princess Viktoria. If Cam couldn't accept both parts of her then the fairy tale ending she dreamed of was impossible.

She had thought he might fight for her—she'd *wanted* him to fight for her—but perhaps she had built a fantasy around him. His commitment to his family and his career made her think he was a strong, dependable person and his strength appealed to her, but he didn't want the Princess.

She had enjoyed almost every minute of her adventure but now she had to leave. Just like Cinderella, it was time for her to go but she didn't think her Prince was going to come after her. Not this time.

CHAPTER TEN

VIKTORIA HAD ONE final check of her reflection in the mirror and readjusted her tiara before making her way down the palace corridors to her mother's wing. She took a deep breath and knocked on her mother's door. She ran her hands over the skirt of her ball gown, nervously smoothing out creases even though she knew Brigitta had steamed every last one out of the pale pink dress. The sleeveless floor-length gown had a fitted bodice with a silk underlay and a flowing chiffon skirt. The dress had been embroidered with hundreds of tiny flowers, each of which had a crystal stitched into its centre that shone and sparkled with every movement. It was stunning, a gown fit for a princess, but Viktoria barely noticed. She was too nervous.

Tonight was the gala ball to mark her father's twenty-five years on the throne. It was the penultimate night of a week of celebrations and Viktoria knew that Tomas, the Duke of San Fernando, would be in attendance. Tomas was her parents' choice as the man deemed worthy of their daughter's hand in marriage and Viktoria had known him since they were children; she supposed that was somewhat comforting. But less comforting was the fact that he was not who she would have chosen to marry.

A couple of months ago she had told Freddie that, of the men on her parents' shortlist, Tomas was her preference. But that had been before she'd met Campbell.

Her thoughts returned to Sydney, as they had done so often over the past week. Back to Cam.

That wasn't helpful.

That had been nothing but a holiday romance, but she hadn't been able to get him out of her head. Granted, she'd been home for less than a week, but this was not the right frame of mind to be accepting another man's proposal when her head and heart belonged to another.

But she was never going to have that opportunity again. It was best just to move on.

Marie, her mother's lady-in-waiting, opened the door and Viktoria stepped into her mother's suite, ready to be reminded of her duty.

'You look lovely, my darling,' her mother greeted her. 'Are you looking forward to seeing Tomas again?'

'*Oui.*'

'And you will accept a proposal of marriage from him?'

Viktoria fought back the feeling of dread, of missed opportunity. She was tempted to say no, but she was a dutiful daughter, a dutiful princess, and she would do her duty as she'd promised. It was not as if she had another option, she thought as she nodded her agreement.

'I am glad,' her mother said. 'Your father and I thought he would be a suitable match. You've known each other since you were children and he is a sensible, good-looking man.'

Viktoria wanted passionate, not sensible. She wanted someone who took her breath away when he smiled, who made her feel like she could dissolve when his lips brushed hers, when he took her in his arms. She wanted to be with someone who made her feel alive. She wanted to be with someone who needed her—Viktoria—to complete them and who completed her.

She didn't bother arguing her case. What was the point? That door had closed. She had made a promise and she would do her duty.

She nodded her agreement. He was a sensible choice. 'Do you know the role I will be expected to play as the Duchess?' She had given this a lot of thought over the past week, when she hadn't been thinking about Cam, and she was eager to get started on some charitable events. If she could put plans in place before she married, then she might have more autonomy. 'I do not want to just hand out trophies and cut ribbons.'

'I imagine you'll start a family.'

'I'm fifth in line to the throne now; I don't have to have children right away.' Her eldest brother had produced heirs and she didn't want to think about having a family just yet. She wanted time to get used to being a married woman. 'Philippe, Nicolas and Philippe's sons are all ahead of me.'

'Tomas will probably want children though, and what else would you do?'

She could think of so many things. 'Being part of the Legion's Games and seeing Freddie's involvement, I've been thinking about starting a charity,' she said.

'You and Tomas can work that out together. He's very involved in several charities. Perhaps you could assist him.'

She didn't want to assist Tomas; she wanted to be in charge. But she knew that wasn't how things worked. Hers would be the supporting role, not the other way around. But she wanted to be an equal. She wanted to feel that her voice was heard.

Marie came back, knocking on the door. 'His Royal Highness has asked if you are ready to join him in the ballroom.'

Viktoria pasted a smile on her face as she followed her mother downstairs and prepared to spend the evening making small talk with her father's guests——as she prepared to endure her last night of freedom before she became engaged to a man she barely knew. Although she had known Tomas since they were children, she'd seen him only a handful of times in the past fifteen years. He was virtually a stranger.

She had barely known Cam either, yet that hadn't stopped her from imagining all sorts of alternative futures.

She had to stop thinking about Campbell. About how easy and simple things had been. About how she'd felt she could be herself. She knew he would argue that she hadn't been. That she was a princess, not a commoner. But she hadn't felt common. She'd felt alive. Happy. Free.

She didn't want a life dictated by royal protocol. She'd imagined a whole other life for herself. In Australia. With Cam. But obviously that wasn't going to be her future.

Maybe she should just accept her fate and the husband her parents had chosen for her.

Perhaps she should try to imagine a future with Tomas. He deserved that chance.

She would try to be open to the possibility that he could be a good match for her, that she could grow to love him.

Viktoria knew the evening was a success. Her mother's meticulous organisational skills were at their peak arranging functions like this and she never settled for anything less than perfection. The palace ballroom was filled with royalty, celebrities, politicians and family and their tiaras, dresses, medals and jewels sparkled under the lights of dozens of chandeliers. Champagne flowed as white-coated staff seamlessly moved around the guests passing out myriad hors d'oeuvres. The band were excellent, and the dance floor was full.

Viktoria accepted each dance that was requested of her, although she made sure to stay close to the band where the music was louder and made conversation difficult. It was easier to dance than to talk.

As she thanked her dance partner at the conclusion of a song Tomas appeared beside her.

'*Bonsoir*, Your Highness.' He bowed slightly and held out a hand. 'May I have the next dance?'

'*Bonsoir,* Tomas, *comme-va?*' she said as she placed her hand in his, accepting his invitation.

He was taller than her, slightly balding. Blond, not dark. Angular, not handsome but pleasant-looking.

She knew she was comparing him to Cam and she knew that was unfair. No one was going to measure up to Cam. And she was well aware too, as Tomas placed his hand on her hip, that there was no spark, no nervous excitement, no anticipation of something bigger. She wasn't being swept off her feet, nor did she feel even remotely as if she might dissolve while he held her in his arms.

She closed her eyes and imagined she was in Cam's embrace. Imagined the warmth of his hand, the touch of his fingers on her skin. She felt disloyal but she couldn't stop herself. This was not what she wanted for herself, for her life, but she couldn't figure out how to get out of it.

Tomas was talking. It was hard to pretend she was in Cam's arms when all she could hear was the sound of another man's voice. She opened her eyes and forced herself to concentrate, to be the perfect hostess she'd been raised to be. *'Pardon?'*

'I was saying how excited I am for you to see the house I have purchased for us.'

'You have purchased a house?' she asked, dampening down her dismay that he'd done so without her approval, without her permission. Would she be allowed a say in anything?

'Yes.'

'Where is it?'

'San Fernando.'

She hadn't envisaged that. She had pictured them living in Berggrun. She'd pictured *herself* living in Berggrun, she realised. She hadn't actually pictured herself living with Tomas. She wondered if her parents had given their approval for her to move away.

Why wouldn't they? She probably wasn't expected to live in Berggrun for ever. But if that was the case why couldn't she live anywhere she liked? In Australia, for example?

'I thought you might like to visit next week,' Tomas was saying. 'Once our engagement is official. It is a blank canvas; I thought you would like to decorate it.'

She tried to picture the sort of house he might choose but all she could imagine was an airy white house perched on top of a cliff. Cam's house.

'It's a big house,' Tomas added. 'It will keep you busy for quite a while.'

She made a non-committal sound, struggling to be enthusiastic, as Tomas guided her confidently around the dance floor. She wanted more for herself than to spend her days decorating. Between the heads and shoulders of the other couples she caught a glimpse of a dark-haired man and, for a moment, she thought it was Campbell but, before she could get a proper look, Tomas had turned her around and she'd lost sight of him.

She told herself she was imagining things but that didn't stop her from searching the edges of the dance floor and the corners of the ballroom as Tomas spun her around.

On one pass she saw Freddie. She hadn't realised he was going to be back from Australia in time for the ball, but it was the man standing beside her cousin, watching her, that caused her to stumble.

He was here.

Cam was here.

'Are you all right?' Tomas asked. He held her a little more firmly and managed to keep her on her feet.

Viktoria was breathing quickly. Her heart was racing. She stood with Tomas in the middle of the dance floor as she stared across the room. Her brain had frozen.

'I think I need some water,' she managed to stammer.

'Of course. Come. Take a seat.' Tomas guided her from the floor to a seat several metres from where Freddie and Cam stood. 'I'll bring you a drink.'

She was barely aware of Tomas leaving her side. Her eyes didn't leave Cam. She held her breath as he came towards her. She didn't blink, couldn't blink. She was terrified that if she closed her eyes, even for a second, he would disappear.

She still wasn't certain if she was imagining things but now here he was, standing in front of her.

She wanted to throw herself into his arms, to feel his embrace, to make sure he was real. But while that was what she would have done if they were in Sydney it was not the way a princess behaved.

She looked from Cam to Freddie, trying to make sense of what she was seeing, and realised she wanted to cry. She wasn't sure why. She thought she was happy. She *was* happy to see him, but she wasn't sure what his appearance meant.

She stood up and kissed Freddie on both cheeks, all without taking her eyes off Cam.

Freddie stepped back and Cam reached for Viktoria's hand. Heat shot through her and she thought her knees might give way as her insides dissolved in a pool of delicious anticipation. She was overwhelmed by all the sensations that she had been longing to feel. Just one look from Cam was enough to melt her, let alone the touch of his hand.

He lifted her hand to his lips and kissed her fingers. 'Hello, Viktoria.'

Hearing her name on his lips, just her name, not *Your Highness* or *Princess*, was the sweetest sound. She'd missed being that person. She'd missed him. It had been less than a week, but it felt like a lifetime.

'Cam… What are you doing here?'

'I've come for you.'

'For me?' Her voice was husky and the room was swimming slightly. She really did need a drink but the last thing she wanted was to still be standing there, with Cam, when Tomas returned.

She swayed on her feet and Cam caught her at the elbow, steadying her. Her skin was on fire. Her head was spinning.

She looked to Freddie. She didn't know what to do.

'Go. I'll keep Tomas occupied,' he said.

Viktoria didn't argue. She took Freddie's cue and slipped through one of the glass doors that were set into the arches along one side of the ballroom. She wanted to take Cam's hand, but she knew she had to wait until she was sure no one was watching them. She probably shouldn't be leaving the ballroom with Cam; in fact she knew she *definitely* shouldn't be doing this—there were rules, lots of rules—but sometimes they just had to be broken.

The glass doors opened onto a large flag-stoned patio. Potted conifers and several clusters of chairs were arranged around the space but there were also a few secluded seating areas tucked under arbours. Discreet gas heaters took the chill out of the late autumn air. She led Cam to a corner of the patio where they were out of sight of the guests in the ballroom.

She perched on a small cushioned seat and reached for his hand, pulling him down to sit beside her. The spot she had chosen overlooked the ocean and far below them the lights of hundreds of boats docked in the marina shone like handfuls of stars scattered across the water. But Viktoria wasn't interested in looking at any of that. Fairy lights strung over the arbour twinkled above them, giving her just enough light to take in Cam's features. She stared at him, recalling every feature, as if afraid something might have changed in the past few days. But he looked as gorgeous as always.

Tall, dark and still incredibly handsome. As perfect in a tuxedo as he'd been in his army fatigues.

'When did you arrive? How? Why?' Her head was still spinning, and his presence made no sense.

'About an hour ago. I came with Prince Alfred. The Palace was keen to have the services of a doctor on board the flight from Australia as a precaution following surgery. He was fine but it was a long flight and he suggested I might like to come with him. I was happy to accompany him, but I really came to see you.'

'But I cannot spend time with you. Tonight is the one night when I have obligations.'

Cam was only semi-aware of his surroundings, of the palace with its view over the marina, of the fairy lights and conifers, but it was all overshadowed by Viktoria. She was breathtakingly beautiful, outshining everything and everyone else. She tugged on his hand and pulled him down to sit beside her.

'I would have come sooner,' he said, 'but I didn't know if you'd want to see me. I didn't realise what I was losing until you had gone and then I figured I couldn't just walk up to the palace unannounced, and knock on the door asking for you. Prince Alfred offered me the opportunity to come with him and I realised I'd always regret it if I didn't take the chance to see if I could rectify the mistake I'd made.'

Cam knew Viktoria had a duty tonight as a hostess. He hadn't even planned on staying long. Prince Alfred had assured him he would get him into the ball and Cam's intention had simply been to let Viktoria know he was in Berggrun. That he had come to see her, and then he was happy to wait until tomorrow.

'I was stubborn and confused and I should

not have let you leave. I needed you to know that, to know that I have come for you. But I will wait. I will wait until tomorrow. I will wait for as long as it takes for you to hear what I have to say.'

'Tell me now.'

'I came to Berggrun to tell you that I don't expect you to give your life up for me. I was foolish. I didn't want to let you down. I didn't think you needed someone like me in your life. I'm still not sure if you do, but I needed to find out one way or the other. You pushed me out of my comfort zone, and I didn't handle that well. Since the incident I prefer my life to be controlled. I don't like unexpected changes. When you arrived, you disturbed my life and my first reaction was to resist, to shut down. I wanted my life to be smooth. I didn't want the unexpected. But then I realised that my life would be boring. Your speech at the Games reminded me not to be afraid. I didn't want to think I might never see you again. If I did nothing I was being cowardly. If I did nothing I was going to miss out on life. On experiences. On you. That is why I am here.

'For you.

'I want you to come back to Australia

with me. Or I will stay here. I don't mind. I just want to be with you. I want to be happy.'

'I want you to be happy too. I want us both to be happy, but you are too late.'

'Please, I'm begging you for a chance.'

'No, you do not understand. You are too late. It is too late for us. Things have changed.'

'What things? It's only been a few days.'

'Tomorrow I will be engaged to be married.'

'What did you say?' Cam was certain he had misheard her. He blamed jet lag.

'I am getting married.'

'Married? To whom?' His stomach churned as he waited for her reply. He fought back a wave of nausea.

'The Duke of San Fernando.'

Who the hell was that?

'When was this decided?' he asked as he picked up her hand. Her ring finger was bare. 'You're not engaged yet.'

'No, but it is all arranged. There is a banquet tomorrow to announce the engagement.'

'Tomorrow?' His heart sunk in his chest, coming to rest like a lump of lead in his gut. 'Are you in love with this guy?'

'I like him. I hope we could have a good life together.'

'You *like* him? What the hell does that mean?'

'It means I have an agreement with my parents, and they made the arrangements.'

'Arrangements? You're talking about an *arranged* marriage? Who in the world still does that?'

'We do. I am expected to marry by the time I am thirty. It is a Berggruner tradition. It is my duty.'

'And then what?' He was horrified. 'You'll spend your days handing out trophies and opening hospitals? I thought you said you wanted more than that.'

'I do. And I thought I could have more, but I made a promise to my parents before I went to Australia. I am running out of time.'

'I thought you were coming back to attend a party, to celebrate your father's twenty-fifth anniversary as Prince; you never said anything about a fiancé, arranged or otherwise.'

'I did not think it mattered any more. Our relationship was done.'

'I came here to see if there was a way forward for us…'

'I am sorry, Cam,' she said as his heart

broke into tiny fragments. 'I made a promise. There is nothing I can do. It is my duty.'

She had healed his heart only to shatter it all over again.

The rest of the night passed in a blur for Viktoria. Cam had requested a last dance, but she turned him down. She had no choice. She was afraid she wouldn't be able to hide how she felt about him. That she wouldn't be able to conceal her love for him and she couldn't broadcast her feelings to the world. Not in front of Tomas, her parents or the press.

Cam had left the ball and Viktoria felt that she was losing her mind. She couldn't focus; her head was full of thoughts of Cam and she was consumed with dread. Was she making a mistake? She was certain she was, but she didn't know how to rectify it.

She knew she needed to see him again. She couldn't let him go without one more goodbye but there was nothing she could do tonight.

She slept fitfully, tossing and turning while she debated her options, before finally deciding she would need to enlist Freddie's help. She didn't know where Cam was staying, she hadn't thought to ask, but she was sure Freddie would. She'd need to call Cam, to ask him to come back to the palace. She would have gone to him but she was wary of the paparazzi. She knew there were rumours that her engagement was about to be announced and speculation about who she would be marrying. She couldn't lead the press to Cam, and she couldn't leave Tomas exposed. She couldn't risk bringing dishonour to him or her parents.

Freddie gave Viktoria the details of Cam's hotel and her heart was pounding as she dialled the number, only to have her hopes and dreams dashed when she was told that he had already checked out.

He was gone.

She was too late.

She couldn't believe what she'd done. She couldn't believe she'd let him go.

She felt sick. What was she going to do now?

Before she could figure that out Brigitta appeared to let her know her parents had requested her company for breakfast.

Viktoria felt as though she was sleepwalking as she returned to the patio where her parents were seated. All traces of the ball had been cleared away but she still couldn't help but think that the patio would always be the last place where she had seen Cam.

She was dimly aware of exchanging pleas-
antries with her parents and trying to listen
to their opinions on the ball, but her mind
was primarily filled with her own troubles.
Until her father caught her attention. 'We
want to speak to you about Tomas.'

Viktoria's heart sank like a stone. They
were going to tell her the process for today's
announcement.

'We are concerned that we may have been
too hasty, that Tomas might not be the right
choice for you,' her mother added.

Viktoria frowned as she tried to translate
her mother's meaning. 'Are you giving me
more time? I am almost thirty.'

'A tradition isn't set in stone,' her father
replied. 'Things can change. Your mother
and I thought you were happy to let us sug-
gest a partner for you after what happened
with Luca. But the choice is yours. If you're
not certain, you can wait.'

'Is it true you met someone in Sydney?'
her mother asked.

'How did you know that? Did Freddie tell
you?'

Her mother nodded. 'Is he someone special?'

'*Oui.*' Viktoria couldn't keep the smile
from her face at the thought of Cam, until

she remembered that she had no idea where he had gone.

'We think you should discuss your situation with him. We want you to be positive you are making the right decision.'

'I do not know if it could work, *how* it could work.'

'There's no way to be certain of everything in life but if you want something badly enough, if it's worth something to you, then you have to try. Do you love him?'

Viktoria thought of the way Cam made her feel. The way she felt when he kissed her. When he held her hand. When he made love to her. When he opened his heart to her.

How she felt when she had to say goodbye. 'I do.'

'Then you need to speak to him again before you make your decision.'

'Do I have your permission?' she asked her father.

'Of course. And our blessing. Now, go to him, talk to him.'

'I don't know where he is.' The realisation felt like a physical blow, knocking the air from her lungs and squeezing her heart in her chest.

'I'm right here.'

She spun around, thinking she must have

imagined his voice, and saw Cam standing behind her.

'Cam!'

She stepped into his arms, reacting on instinct, without hesitation. 'I rang your hotel. They told me you had checked out. I thought you had gone.'

His arms enclosed her, and she was only vaguely aware of her parents leaving the patio, leaving her alone with Cam.

'I couldn't leave,' he told her. 'Not without you. Last night I had to respect the fact that you had a duty as a hostess. I wasn't about to create drama but, until you are officially engaged to someone else, I'm not prepared to accept that what we had is over. I spent the night figuring out what to do, figuring out where we go from here, and now I need to speak to you.' He took her hand and led her back to the same seat where they had sat last night.

He sat down and pulled her into his lap. 'I should never have let you go but I didn't feel I was right for you. I didn't think I had anything to offer you. I was angry and sad at the same time and riddled with guilt. I was scarred. Although my physical wounds had healed, I still bore my emotional ones. I felt broken, cracked open, exposed and vulner-

able but when I was with you I felt myself
healing. You were a balm to my soul, and
you showed me a path to a future where I
thought I could be happy again, but I wasn't
sure if I could make you happy. And I didn't
think I could compete with your duty as a
royal. But then I realised I didn't want to
compete. I love you and I want to support
you. If you'll have me. I don't want to lose
you. I don't want you to marry someone else.
I want you to marry me.'

She had wanted him to fight for her. To
come for her.

And he had.

'You want to marry me?'

'Yes. And I'm not leaving without you.'

'What if I can't leave?'

'Well, then, I'll figure out a way to stay
here. I have always liked to make plans, but I
stopped after Gemma died. When I met you
I started thinking ahead again, planning a
future, not knowing you were a princess, not
knowing you had a duty to Prince and country. I didn't think I could compete against
that. I thought I would lose you to your duty,
just like I had lost Gemma, and I figured
there was nothing I could do. But this time
I can do something. And I am going to fight
for what I want. And what I want is you. If

there is any way to make this work, I will do it. I was never the type of person who gave up and I am not prepared to give up on us. I haven't lost you yet. There's still a chance. But that is up to you.'

He reached out and wiped a tear from her cheek. She hadn't even realised she was crying. But they were happy tears. He hadn't left without her. He loved her.

'I understand you have a duty as a princess,' he said, 'and I can live with that. I'm not asking you to give that up for me, but I'm not prepared to lose you to another man.'

'Do you think you could live here? In Berggrun.'

'I have no idea,' he said with a smile. 'I haven't seen anything of it yet except for a palace and a hotel room. Will you show me around?'

'Yes—' she smiled in return '—I would love to.'

'I'm glad. But first there is something else I need to ask you.' He lifted her off his lap and put her on the seat. He got down on one knee. 'I didn't think I had anything to offer you, but I can offer you my love. Viktoria, I love you. Will you marry me?'

Her smile stretched even wider as she reached for his hands. 'You have plenty to offer me,' she said. 'You are also kind, loyal, intelligent and the sexiest man I have ever met, and I love you. I want to be more than a princess. I want to be your wife and, yes, I will marry you.'

It seemed that fairy tale endings were real after all, she thought as he kissed her.

* * * * *